RETURN
— OF THE —
SERAPH

CRAIG UNGRUHN

PAGE PUBLISHING, INC.
Conneaut Lake, PA

First originally published by Page Publishing 2021

ISBN 978-1-6624-2874-6 (pbk)
ISBN 978-1-6624-2875-3 (digital)

Printed in the United States of America

PROLOGUE

Part 1: Approximately
Three Hundred Years Ago

SINCE THE VERY beginning, mankind has always been in constant struggle. Humans are always competing for fame, power, and wealth. This led them to create new technology, trying to outperform the competition and make their lives easier.

However, this new technology came at a very steep price. It required the use of natural resources to build and maintain, of which there was a limited supply. The humans kept constantly making new inventions, never thinking what might happen should this supply run out.

And then, there's the matter of pollution. The technology they created caused vast amounts of harmful chemicals to be released into the environment. These chemicals poisoned the land, sea, and air of their home planet, known as Earth. The humans knew of the harm that their technology caused to the planet but never thought that it could do any major harm to the planet.

But they were wrong. Eventually, the toxic chemicals released by their machines polluted the planet so much that the planet became uninhabitable. The land would not yield any crops, the water caused all who drank it to fall terribly ill, and the air would choke anyone who breathed it.

Eventually, the humans learned of the damage that they had caused to the planet, but by then, it was too late to stop it or fix it. They learned that the planet that they had called home for many millennia would no longer be able to sustain them. All the governments of Earth came together, united for the first time in history, to figure out how to save the human race from extinction. They decided that they would have to find a new home, a new planet that they could live on.

Working quickly, the humans built hundreds of rockets capable of traveling millions of miles through space. At the same time, astronomers began searching all over the galaxy for a planet that could sustain them. There was only one livable planet that they could find, just close enough for their rockets to reach. When all of the rockets were ready, they loaded food, water, and some machines that they would need to start a life on the new planet, then they loaded several billion humans onto the rockets and launched them into space.

However, not everyone got to go onto these rockets. There were not enough rockets to hold every person and not enough time to build more rockets. So several trillion humans were left behind on their toxic planet. These humans suffered a horrible fate, having been left to die a slow, agonizing death because of starvation, illness, suffocation, or from the many wars that broke out over control of what little resources were left on the planet. Over the next fifty years, the population on Earth began dwindling until all life on the planet eventually died. The planet then became a desolate, inhospitable wasteland.

Those that were chosen to leave the planet had a long journey ahead of them. The rockets were capable of reaching the planet but would not do so for many years. They spent several decades on these shuttles, waiting for the day when they would get to see their new home. Many grew increasingly restless, and some even went insane on the journey. Fights often broke out, and some didn't survive the journey.

Eventually, the rockets reached their destination, the planet that the humans would call their new home, Haven. The shuttles slowly descended down onto the planet, one by one. As the touched the planet surface, the large doors on the side of each shuttle opened slowly, and the humans tentatively walked out onto the surface of the planet. They looked with awe and wonder at this new world. They took in the sights, sounds, smells, and everything else that this planet had to offer. One thing that they noticed about Haven was that it was remarkably similar to Earth. The atmosphere and environment of this new planet was almost identical to that of their own planet. Even the wildlife was very similar to theirs.

Eventually, the humans crossed paths with a race of native creatures that they called seraph. They looked and acted just like humans, except they were much stronger, faster, and more intelligent. At first, the two races had difficulty communicating with one another due to speaking a different language, but the seraph were able to study human speech and behavior and eventually learned how to speak their various different languages.

The humans told the seraph their story and asked them to allow humans and seraph to live on the planet together. The seraph refused, saying that if the humans destroyed their own planet, then they would likely destroy this one as well. This caused the humans to panic, as they could find no other planet capable of sustaining them. In their panic, the humans began thinking that the only way to ensure their survival was to eliminate the seraph. Humans have always been a very violent race.

And so the humans secretly began building homes and living off the land on the planet. They then began creating weapons to use against the seraph. When the seraph eventually found out about this, they were furious. They began attacking the human settlements to try to force them off the planet. The humans began fighting back with the weapons that they had developed, and a decades-long war broke out between the two races. The seraph were physically and intellectually superior to humans, but the humans far outnumbered the seraph, who only had a few thousand inhabitants. The war was brutal, and millions of humans were killed in the fighting, but the humans were able to hunt the seraph down and destroy their settlements. Eventually, the humans found the last seraph settlement and wiped out all of them that remained.

However, the humans let three of them live so that they could be studied. Two male and one female seraph were captured and taken to a top-secret facility the humans had developed. There, they performed cruel experiments on the seraph to better understand their biology. Eventually, the seraph were frozen and their bodies were kept in cryogenic stasis, but they were all still alive. The humans discovered that the seraph had an astoundingly long life span, able to live for several thousand years. The seraph bodies were given to the three most powerful nations on the planet, one for each of them.

After the war was over, the humans began to rebuild the settlements that were destroyed and build new settlements. The process was slow and difficult, but over the next several centuries, the humans built towns and cities all over the planet. Many nations were formed from all the different cultures and races of humans. They started to rebuild the technology that they had on Earth, and over the next three centuries, their technological capabilities advanced until it reached the same point that it had when they left Earth. They created automobiles, electricity, phones, Internet, and advanced weaponry. At first, they lived in peace, working together to build a new life on their new home. However, this peace did not last long, for just as they had fought on Earth, so they also fought on Haven.

PROLOGUE

Part 2: Thirty Years Ago

ALEX AND SARA Branford were a simple couple living in the country-side of the nation known as Excellus, founded by the inhabitants of the Earth nation known as the United States of America. They had been married for about ten years. Alex was a mechanic who mostly fixed cars, a burly man with short, black hair and tan skin, while Sara was a manager at a local grocery store, a short, slender woman with long, blond hair. They were both in their late twenties. They never had a lot of money, but they always made enough to get by and be happy.

One day, the couple went out with friends at a local club. They were there for several hours, having a fun time, and eventually decided to go back home at about 10:00 p.m. (on Haven, days were longer than they were on Earth; where Earth days were twenty-four hours long, a day on Haven lasted thirty-two hours, meaning that the day ended at 16:00 p.m.). As they were driving back home, they noticed something peculiar on the side of the road. They pulled into a ditch and got out of their truck. As they made their way through the ditch, they could hear cries coming from a baby. Sure enough, they found an abandoned baby not far from the truck.

Alex calls to Sara, "Come over here! You need to see this!"

Sara made her way to Alex's side and looked at the infant in front of him. "What is it doing here?" she asked.

Alex replied, "I don't know. Its mother must have left it here."

"Why would anybody do that to a poor, helpless child?"

"I don't know, but we can't just leave it here. We need to help it."

"You want to take it with us?"

"You've been saying for years that you want a child. Well, now's our chance to have a kid of our own."

"But can we take care of a child?"

"Look, let's just take him back to our house, and we can decide what to do with him when we get there." Alex picked up the child and held it tightly in his arms. The child was a boy, weighing about four pounds, and very young, probably less than a year old. It had black hair, but there was very little of it. Its eyes were bright green, a very strange shade, but Alex thought little of it. Alex and Sara got back into their truck, and Sara drove them home as Alex held the child in the passenger seat. The drive took about twenty minutes, and the entire time Alex and Sara were silent, contemplating what this would mean for them.

When the truck reached their home, Sara pulled it into the driveway and into the garage, shutting the door behind them. Sara and Alex got out of the truck and took the still-crying baby inside. Alex went into the bathroom to wash the dirt off of the baby's body and dried it with a nearby towel. He then wrapped the towel around the child's body and took him into the kitchen, where Sara was sitting at the table quietly. Alex took a seat at the table and handed the infant to Sara, who cradled it in here arms and slowly swayed it back and forth. This made the baby stop crying, and it soon closed its eyes and drifted off to sleep. Sara let out a sigh of relief at this, while she continued to slowly sway the child.

"So what do we do now?" asked Alex.

"I don't know. Do you think we should keep it?" Sara questioned back.

"I think so. There's nowhere else for the kid to go. We can't just get rid of it."

"We could put it up for adoption. There's an adoption clinic in Columbia—it's not very far away."

"I thought you wanted a child? That's what you've been telling me ever since we got married."

"I know, but I'm not sure if this is the right time."

"When will the right time be?" Alex got out of his seat and stood beside Sara, looking down at the child in her arms.

Sara responded, "I don't know. This whole situation is just so strange. I don't really know what to make of it."

"Look, we will be just fine. I can go to the store tomorrow and get some things. You just stay here and take care of the child."

"Oh, all right. I suppose we can take care of it. But if we are going to keep this child, we should give it a name."

"How about Zack?"

"I… I like that." Sara looked down at the child again. "Zack Branford…that's a very nice name."

Alex and Sara stayed up all night; the child slept soundly throughout the whole night. During that time, they wrote a list of all of the items that they would need from the store.

When morning came, Alex drove his truck into a nearby town, called Pleasance, and went into the local grocery store. There, he bought all of the items on the list: food, clothes, diapers, a crib, etc. He walked out of the store and to his truck, where he put all the items in the back. He then drove the truck home, arriving about twenty minutes later. He took all the items out of the back of the truck and took them inside his house, where Sara was now sitting in the living room, still cradling the child in her arms.

"Did you get everything?" Sara asked as Alex walked into the living room.

"Yeah," Alex answered quickly.

"All right, so just put the food on the counter, put the diapers and wipes in the bathroom, and put everything else in the guest room."

Alex did all of this, set up the crib in the guest room, put a pillow and blanket in it, and put the child's clothes in the closet in the room.

After about ten minutes, he finished this and returned to the living room to see that the child had awoken. Sara smiled at Alex as he walked into the room and began playing with the child. Now Alex's face turned into a large grin as he watched.

Sara said to Alex, "I think I'm glad that we decided to keep this child. I just wonder who abandoned him in a ditch."

Alex responded, "We'll probably never know. But that doesn't matter now. All that matters is that we give this child a good home."

"I suppose you're right. Do you think we will make good parents?"

"I know we will. I don't know anyone else who would make a better mother than you."

Sara and Alex then continued playing with the baby, wondering how it got to be with them, and contemplating the future that they will have with it.

Over the next eighteen years, Alex and Sara raised Zack as their own child. He went to a nearby public school, where he excelled. He was very intellectually gifted, getting all As throughout elementary, middle, and high school. He was also very physically gifted, having been in multiple sports and excelling in all of them. Sara and Alex never told Zack how they found him because they thought that it would be emotionally scarring for him, so throughout his entire childhood, Zack thought that Alex and Sara were his biological parents.

After finishing high school, Zack decided that he wanted to join the military, specifically the marines. He passed the physical evaluation and basic training with ease, passing at the top of his class. The area that he excelled at most was in close-quarters combat, able to defeat all his classmates in every single encounter.

His weapon of choice, therefore, was a sword. It was custom-made for him, with a blade that was five-and-a-half feet long, slightly curved in the center, and made of a rare metal found only on Haven called insolubilis (the strongest metal known to exist, much stronger than any metal on Earth). The blade had a silvery color, and it glistened brightly in light. The hilt was about two feet in length (so it could be held with two hands), with a circular guard, and it was made out of a plastic-like substance found on Haven called alund (a soft substance that is easily moldable, it undergoes a hardening process for certain uses). The sword came with a black holder that strapped around the user's waist to allow for quick sheathing and unsheathing. It was also made out of alund. The design for the sword was modeled after the katana, and it was incredibly durable, and its sharpness was rivaled by few other blades. This type of sword was very rare, with only about three thousand of them in the entire world; therefore, it was only given to the very best recruits, and Zack was one of them.

Zack was very impressed with his new weapon. He carried the sword everywhere he went, taking great pride in it. He trained daily with it, practicing and perfecting new techniques and practicing his other combat skills.

However, Zack was also very skilled with other weapons as well. He often practiced with the use of firearms; pistols, rifles, and shotguns. He used these weapons in many battles when necessary. He usually carried a pistol around his waist along with his sword. His pistol of choice was one that was modeled after the Desert Eagle, featuring a triangular barrel about ten inches long, a magazine capacity of twenty bullets that fired .50 caliber rounds, and a black coating of paint. It weighed about five pounds and was about fifteen inches in length. It was semi-automatic, capable of firing around twenty rounds per minute, and it had a range of about three hundred meters. Although the weapon was capable of having multiple different sights attached to it, Zack preferred to use the iron sights of the weapon, as he usually used it against targets at close range. The weapon had a large amount of recoil, and although most people had a difficult time firing it, Zack never had any trouble handling it. The weapon was named the Desert Fox.

Zack was in military training for two years before he was called into active service. Excellus had high tensions with several nations, and these tensions with one nation eventually led to war with the nation of Imperia. Zack's unit was one of the first sent into battle. He saw much combat over the course of the seven-year conflict, distinguishing himself due to his battle prowess. He led many successful missions and quickly rose through the ranks of the military. Eventually, thanks in part to Zack's skills in combat and leadership, Excellus won the war, and with the victory, Excellus gained much power and prestige. Zack earned many awards and commendations for his efforts. He rose through the ranks faster than most soldiers, and became a colonel by the end of the conflict, where he had command over dozens of soldiers.

Zack had to sleep in a barrack on nights when he wasn't on a mission with about twenty other men. On most nights, he had a lot of trouble sleeping, and when he did sleep, he had strange dreams about a mysterious woman talking to him. He never knew what to make of these dreams, and he never told anyone about them.

After the war with Imperia was over, Zack trained for many years to work in health and safety, wanting to leave behind his past in the war because of the things he experienced. He was then reassigned to be a health inspector for a number of top-secret government facilities. He tested all of these facilities to know if they were operating safely according to what the government required. Most of the time, they were, especially the high-class facilities. However, he occasionally had to report code violations and other such problems, which usually led to someone getting fired and a strict probationary period for that facility. Zack enjoyed his work very much, as it allowed him to travel all over the nation and see many new things.

CHAPTER 1

Modern Day

ZACK GETS READY for his next assignment, inspecting a base in the northern district of the country, a high-security, top-secret facility used to research weapons for the military. He puts on his work uniform, which consists of black khakis, a white shirt, and his white tennis shoes in his bedroom. His bedroom is small, consisting of white walls, a regular-sized bed in the center, a dresser to the right of it, and a closet in the far right corner of the room. His entire house was of a similar layout, small and plain. Once he is dressed, he puts his wallet and phone into his pocket.

He then goes into his bathroom, where he shaves his chin and sideburns, brushes his teeth, and combs his hair. His hair has grown long enough that it now reaches his shoulders, and he combs the back so that it sits flatly on his head, and the front he combs so that it flows down to the right of his face. He inspects himself in the large mirror for a few seconds before deciding that he looks good enough to go out on assignment.

Once that is finished, he heads out the door into the garage, where his old car is parked. The garage, like the rest of the house, is rather small, containing only one vehicle, tan walls, and, in the corner, a few tools that he uses from time to time, as well as an old grill. The car is about eight years old, with four doors, a rather large body for a car, and dark blue paint. The inside has tan leather seats and a radio that barely works. Zack makes a relatively large income working for the government, but he rarely spends any money except on food, clothes, and paying for his house and car. He could easily afford a much nicer vehicle, but Zack has grown accustomed to the vehicle he has now and refuses to buy a new one unless he absolutely has to.

Zack locks the door into his garage before getting inside the car, putting the key in the ignition, and starting the car. He once again looks at himself in the mirror, checking to make sure he didn't forget anything. Then he opens up the garage door via a button in his car and slowly back out of the garage. After getting out of his driveway, he makes the twenty-minute trip to his office. He turns on the radio in the car, and the faint sound of rock music comes out of the speakers. Zack turns the knob to increase the volume, but it doesn't make the music much louder. Zack listens to it anyway, and he even begins shaking his head to the music whenever a song he likes comes on.

Eventually, Zack arrives at the building where he works, and he turns left into the driveway and drives along the long path to the parking lot. After finding a space, he parks, turns off his car, and gets out of it. As he closes the door, Evan, one of his coworkers, walks up to him to talk.

"Hey, Zack. How's it going?" Evan begins.

"Hey, Evan," Zack answers. "It's going all right. Are you ready for this inspection?"

"Yeah. I can't believe we actually get to go to the Mt. Hormel base. That's hundreds of miles away!"

The Mt. Hormel facility is the most sophisticated military research facility in the entire world. There, scientists, doctors, and weapon experts work tirelessly to develop new weapons and technology for the military. The facility is one of the most secretive and well-guarded places in the world.

Zack replies, "I know. This is going to be very interesting."

"You mean long and stressful, right?"

Zack laughs, "Well, at least the plane ride there and back will be pleasant."

"Oh, I know. The government sure doesn't spare any expense when it comes to these inspections."

"Can you blame them?"

"I guess not. Still, though, it seems rather strange that they would use such high-end planes just to get us to an inspection."

"You're not complaining, are you?"

Evan laughs, "Hell no! If we have to go all the way to the Northern Province, I at least want to go in style."

This time, Zack and Evan both laugh. Once they are finished, Zack looks at his phone and sees that their shift is about to start. He then says to Evan, "Look, we should go inside."

"Yeah, yeah, let's go," Evan replies.

Zack and Evan walk into the large building together via the large door in front. From there, they walk up to the front desk to swipe their employee ID cards and clock in to work. They then walk into the office of their manager and sit down in two of the several chairs placed there. As the minutes go by, more and more people come into the office and sit down, talking among themselves and waiting for the manager to arrive. One of them, named Mike, sits next to Zack.

"Hey, Zack," Mike begins. "How's it going?"

Zack replies, "It's going all right. How about yourself?"

"It's good. So how are things at home?"

"Fine."

"Are you still driving around in that piece of junk you call a car?"

"Oh, really? You're gonna do this again, are you? Well, if you really care that much about it, why don't you buy me a new one?"

Mike laughs at this before saying, "No, no, that's alright. You can keep your piece of shit car. I just don't understand why you still drive that thing. You can easily afford a new car."

Evan interjects, "Maybe it's because unlike you, Zack doesn't feel the need to constantly spend money on everything he sees."

Mike responds, "Well, why not? When you make this much money, you might as well spend it, right?"

Zack replies, "I don't really see the point in buying material goods."

Mike gives Zack a puzzled look before saying, "Whatever. It's your life, even if it is a boring one."

Zack rolls his eyes and turns away just as the manager walks in. He sits down at his desk and gives a short presentation about the Mt. Hormel facility, specifically about the contents and research that goes on at the facility and the security protocols in place. Once he is finished, he says, "All right, the presentation is now over. The rest of the information should be in the e-mail you all received about a week ago. Time to get on the plane and head to the facility. If you want to read through your e-mail again, you will have plenty of time to read them on the plane."

Everyone in the office takes their belongings and goes outside. There, they get into their respective vehicles to drive to the airport. The trip takes about ten minutes, and on the way, Zack listens to more rock music from his radio.

Once at the airport, Zack takes his packet and walks inside to the front desk of the airport. All of his coworkers are already there, waiting to go through security. Zack finds Evan in the crowd and stands next to him.

Evan says to Zack, "This is always the most annoying part of riding on a plane."

Zack replies, "Well, do you want people to just bring whatever they want on these planes?"

"No, but does the process have to take so long?"

"They're just being thorough. With all these lunatics running around nowadays, one can never be too careful."

"Yeah, but it's still tedious as hell."

"Well, there's nothing we can do about it. Complaining about it won't make it go away, so you're just going to have to suck it up."

"Yeah, yeah, I know."

The employees go through the security checkpoint, having to go through numerous scanners. They all pass through without incident and are then boarded onto the plane.

The inside of the plane looks like any other commercial airliner, with white walls and ceiling, grayish carpet placed on the floor, three columns of seats, six seats per row. There are enough seats to hold about forty people, although there are less than twenty passengers right now. The seats are made of tan leather, the armrests are made out of wood, each one having a cup holder. The seats sit about four feet apart in the front and back, giving passengers ample room to stretch out their legs. The plane is owned by the government and, from what Zack knows, is very expensive, even compared to other planes. Like almost all other commercial planes, this one comes with built-in wireless internet.

Zack takes a seat next to Evan on the plane, takes out his phone, and begins going through his e-mail. He has already read it dozens of times, but he wants to read through it again just to be thorough. He knows that he will be handling the main research wing, which is where the most important research at the facility takes place and is also the place where a seraph body is kept. He looks through the e-mail packet quickly before putting his phone to sleep and placing it inside his pocket.

Evan looks at Zack and asks, "So what area are you inspecting?"

Zack answers, "The main research wing."

With a look of surprise, Evan says, "Nice. That's the most important part of the entire facility. Me, I got a much less prestigious part of the facility. I got the sewage system."

Zack wrinkles his nose and says, "Ew. Good luck with that."

"Yeah, tell me about it. Hey, Mike, what place did you get?"

Zack has just noticed that Mike was sitting across the aisle from them.

Mike responds, "I got the medical bay."

Evan says, "Hmm. Not too bad. At least it's a hell of a lot better than what I got."

Mike lets out a low chuckle at this as he continues to look through his packet.

Evan turns back to Zack and says, "This is just great. The *one* time I get to go to Mt. Hormel and I have to spend it looking through shit. Well, this is just going to be a *great* time."

Zack replies, "I'm sorry about your assignment, but you don't have to complain to me about it."

"You're right. I'm sorry, Zack."

Zack rests his head on the chair and lets out a long sigh. He begins to doze off but quickly wakes himself up right before he does. Although the trip will take about three hours, he doesn't want to sleep because he doesn't know when he will wake up, and he has to review the e-mail again later. To not fall asleep, Zack calls the flight attendant and orders a cup of coffee.

Coffee on Haven is not exactly the same as it was on Earth. On this planet, coffee beans are much larger they were on Earth, and instead of being black, they are bright green. As such, coffee has a greenish-yellowish color. The taste is also different, with coffee on Haven usually being much sweeter than on Earth, and as such, a lot less people use sugar in it. However, coffee is still just as popular on Haven as it was on Earth, and it is especially popular in Excellus. It has a lot of caffeine in it, just like coffee on Earth, making it a popular choice for a morning drink to help wake people up. It isn't the same drink as it was on Earth, but the name was kept because it has almost the same properties as the coffee on Earth.

Zack blinks several times and shakes his head to wake himself up. He looks over and sees Evan looking at him.

"Sleepy, are we?" Evan questions.

"I didn't get a whole lot of sleep last night," Zack begins. "So yes, you could say that I am rather tired."

"You're so weird, man."

"What are you talking about?"

"Just the way you talk, the way you act. It's so strange."

"What's so strange about the way I act?"

"You're just so...secretive."

"Did you ever think that maybe I have a good reason for being secretive?"

"What reason would you have for needing to be secretive?"

"It's none of your business."

"Exactly my point."

"Whatever. I don't need to explain myself to you."

Evan shakes his head and lets out a long sigh. He then takes out his phone and starts browsing the Internet with it.

Just then, the flight attendant returns and gives Zack his coffee. It is served in a Styrofoam cup with a lid on it. Zack takes the lid off and smells the coffee. There is a small trail of steam coming off of it. After sniffing the coffee, Zack puts the lid back on and takes a small sip from it. It tastes warm and pleasant, and Zack is filled with a feeling of rejuvenation. He feels much more awake now.

Zack takes his phone out of his pocket and starts browsing the Internet. He looks at the website of a news station close to where he lives. Looking through the various articles on the site, he sees nothing very interesting or noteworthy. After a few minutes of this, he puts his phone to sleep again and puts it back in his pocket before taking another sip from his coffee. He then spends several minutes just sitting in his seat drinking his coffee.

Evan then turns to Zack and says, "Hey, are you doing anything this weekend?"

Zack answers, "No, not really. Why?"

"Well, I was thinking that maybe, if you weren't busy, you could come to my place and we can watch the game. I just got this new TV, and it is amazing. The picture quality on that thing is so good, you will think that you are in the stands yourself. What do you say?"

"It sounds fun. I might have to do that."

"I could also invite a few of my other friends over. We could get a few packs of beer, get some chips—it'll be great."

"Okay. At least I won't have to do anything."

Evan laughs before jokingly saying, "Ah, you lazy bastard. Just for that, I might have you clean up afterward."

Zack laughs at this then takes another sip from his cup of coffee.

Mike then interjects, "Hey, are you guys having a party or something?"

Evan responds, "Were you listening to our conversation?"

"I didn't mean to. I just couldn't help but overhear you guys talking about watching the game this weekend."

"Yeah, we are. What, you want to come too?"

"Kind of, yeah."

"Well, all right. I guess one more person couldn't hurt."

"Thank you kindly."

Zack then asks Evan, "Are you really going to invite that idiot over too?"

Evan answers, "Yeah, sure. He's not that bad."

"Okay, whatever. It's your house."

Zack then takes his phone out again and starts looking through his e-mail. He doesn't have any new e-mails, but he looks through the e-mail from work again to be sure he knows what to do.

After he is finished with that, the pilot's voice comes over the announcements, saying, "This is your captain speaking. We are about to start our landing approach. Please put your seatbelts on and leave them on until the seatbelt light in front of you turns off."

Zack puts his phone to sleep and puts it in his pocket as everyone puts their seatbelts on and a red light turns on in front of all of the seats, displaying the word *seatbelt*. The plane starts descending slowly until it hits the ground and comes to a complete stop a few minutes later. The red light turns off, and everyone takes their seatbelts off.

Then everyone begins standing up and walking out of the plane. As soon as Zack gets off the plane, the first thing that hits him is the cold wind grazing his face. He shivers slightly before getting into the group formed a few feet away. Everyone stands there, waiting a few minutes until several vans arrive to drive everyone to the facility. Zack gets in the closest van and sits in the back left seat. It is a medium-sized van, with four doors and a red exterior. The inside has two seats in the front and six in the back, with grayish leather seats. Evan sits next to him and Mike next to him. Four more people enter the van, filling every seat. The driver then says to them, "Everyone settled in? Put on your seatbelts." The driver is a young man, somewhere in his mid to late twenties, with short black hair. He has a very deep, foreboding voice, reminding Zack of his drill instructor when he was in the military. Zack, Mike, and Evan sit in silence as the van drives for a few minutes until it reaches the base.

Outside the base, there is a large gate barring access to the facility to unauthorized personnel. The driver pulls up next to a guard post next to the base, where the guard says, "Identification, please." The driver and the passengers all hand their ID cards to the guard, who quickly scans them. After a few seconds, the guard hands the cards back to everyone and says, "Proceed." The gate opens, and the driver drives to the second checkpoint, also having a large gate in front of it.

Here, one of the guards stops the vehicle and inspects the outside of it. After about two minutes of this, he also says, "Proceed." The gate opens as the driver goes through it as well.

The driver then reaches the third and final checkpoint, once again having a large gate in front. Here, a guard walks up to the driver and signals him to roll down his window. As the driver does this, the guard says, "Would you all please step out of the vehicle?" Everyone gets out of the van as the guard searches inside it. After about two minutes, the guard says, "You're all free to step back into the vehicle." Everyone gets back in the van as the gate in front of them opens.

The driver drives the van through the gate and into the parking lot, where he drives around to the back of the building and parks in the nearest available space. Everyone gets out of the vehicle again and walks into the front door of the large white building.

CHAPTER 2

THE GROUP WALKS up to the security checkpoint in front of them where a nearby guard gives them instructions. He says, "All right, now, I want you all to walk through this scanner, slowly, one at a time. After that, one of the guards will ask you for your ID card and will direct you to your assigned post. Everyone understand?"

The whole group gives a collective yes and follows the guard's instructions. The driver steps forward first, walking through a tall, white arch with red sensors placed all around its interior. The machine quickly scans him and finds nothing harmful on him, thus it doesn't make any noise. The driver then quickly steps aside as a guard says, "Next," and a young woman with red hair walks through. The machine also finds nothing dangerous on her, and one of the scientists walks over to her, and she gives him her ID card before he says, "Follow me," and leads her to a different area of the building. This same process is repeated for the other five employees.

Zack is the last person in the group to go through the scanner, after which a young woman with short black hair walks up to him, and he hands her his ID card. She examines it for a few seconds before saying, "Follow me." She leads Zack down several hallways, passing through a number of laboratories, all of which have their doors closed so nobody can look inside. After a few minutes of walking, the woman turns to Zack and says, "The main research wing is just through this door." She points to a large white door next to her.

"I will open the door for you, and then someone inside will point you to your first station. All right?"

Zack nods quickly. The woman then walks up to the door, types in a short password onto the keypad next to the door, and swipes her ID card into the scanner attached to it. The door then opens, and Zack walks through it into a large, round room, containing several smaller rooms inside. The walls and ceiling of the room are white, and the floor has a light gray color. As soon as Zack walks in, a young man in a lab coat, goggles, and blue latex gloves walks up to him and says, "This way." He leads Zack to a room just to the right and says, "You're going to need to wear a lab coat, gloves, and safety goggles. They're in that closet," as he points to a closet in the far corner of the room. Zack quickly opens the closet door and puts on the necessary attire.

Afterward, the man says to Zack, "This way please," and leads him to the room right across from the closet. Inside, there is a team of four scientists examining some vials of chemicals; what they are Zack doesn't know.

Snapping back into focus, Zack says, "Oh, sorry. I guess I should actually do my job now, right?"

The man chuckles and replies, "Yeah, I guess so."

Zack then begins examining the room, checking for any chemical spills, making sure all chemicals are labeled and properly stored, and making sure all supplies are in their proper place. After several minutes of searching, Zack finds no violations in the room, and he tells the man, "I think I'm done with this room. Can you take me to the next one?"

"All right," the man answers. "Follow me."

The man leads Zack out of the room and into the next room of his examination. Before that, however, Zack takes off his gloves, washes his hands, takes out his phone, and opens up the e-mail detailing his instructions. Attached to the e-mail is a checklist detailing everything he needs to look for and all of the rooms he needs to check. He opens up the checklist and writes a few notes in the designated space. Once that is finished, Zack puts the phone back in his pocket and puts on a new set of gloves.

Zack steps into the next room, which has no one in it. Just like in the previous room, he checks all around for any leaks, mislabeled containers, etc., and just like the previous room, he finds no violations. So he repeats the process of washing his hands, writing his notes, etc. He does this again for the next several rooms.

Eventually, the man leads Zack into a room with tighter security than the rest. Before entering the room, the man tells Zack, "This is a special room. This is where the body of a seraph is held, so per protocol, you must be even more careful here than in the other rooms."

Zack says, "I am familiar with the protocols about the seraph. It was in the briefing. I'll be careful, don't worry."

"Sorry. It's just that if anything happens to it, then my ass will be gone in a heartbeat. Don't mess anything up, you hear?"

"Yeah, yeah, I hear."

The man enters a password and swipes his keycard into an electronic reader next to the door, causing the large, metal door to open slowly. Zack steps into the room and walks around cautiously. The room is full of strange devices and chemicals that Zack cannot identify, but the most significant part of the room is on the far side, where a large chamber lies. Inside the chamber lies the body of a seraph. The window on the front is partially covered in fog and ice, but most of the body is still visible.

The seraph has large incredibly large muscles, much larger than humans are capable of having, and milky white skin. His hair is very long and flowing, reaching down to his shoulders, with a dark brown color. A small towel is placed over his groin, reaching all the way down to his knees.

After looking at the seraph for a few seconds, Zack continues his work. However, he quickly develops a headache, and it gets worse and worse as he gets closer to the seraph. It is unlike anything he has felt before, and he feels like someone is tearing his head off.

The man sees Zack's strange behavior and eventually asks, "Hey, are you all right?"

Zack's legs begin to feel like jelly, and they give way, causing him to collapse to the floor. The pain gets worse and worse, eventually causing him to pass out. As he lies unconscious, he has another dream of the mysterious woman.

CHAPTER 3

A STREAM OF fog is blown into his face as the door in front of him slowly opens. He opens his eyes slightly, letting in the small amount of light from the room. He has to quickly close them as it is blinding, but he is able to adjust to it. The room is filled with a strange greenish fog, along with shattered glass covering a large portion of the floor. He sees a number of vials thrown onto the floor, shattered, with some leaking fluids of various colors. Slowly, he steps out of the chamber and onto the cold floor of the room. The inside of the room is quiet, but outside, it is complete chaos as people are desperately running to get away. The seraph walks toward the door of the room, careful to avoid stepping on any glass, but a guard soon enters, wearing a gas mask and pointing an assault rifle at him.

"Stop right where you are!" the guard yells at the seraph.

The seraph charges forward and punches the guard in the abdomen, sending him flying several feet backward before hitting the door with a loud clang. Another guard enters, again wearing a gas mask and equipped with an assault rifle. The seraph lifts the guard from his neck and throws him across the room, landing right next to the previous guard. Once again, a guard comes rushing in, only to again be grabbed by the neck and lifted into the air. This time, the seraph snaps the guard's neck with a single hand, killing him instantly. The first guard is dead as well, but the second guard is still writhing on the ground and moaning from the impact of the throw.

As the seraph walks toward him, the guard pleads, "Please, don't kill me. You don't have to kill me."

The seraph disregards these pleas and violently stomps on the guard's head, killing him.

The seraph then walks outside into a long hallway, where sirens are blaring. In the distance, he can hear feet stomping, coming closer to him, probably more guards. He looks at the walls and sees the word *Armory* painted along with an arrow pointing right. He quickly runs in that direction as more guards arrive on the scene.

The captain of the guards witnesses the seraph running away and orders, "After him. That way."

The guards all run in the direction he is pointing, trying to reach the seraph before he can acquire some weapons. They fail.

The seraph reaches the armory and breaks down the large metal door with his bare hands. Inside, he sees a number of wondrous weapons, most of which he cannot discern what they are. However, along the far wall, he sees dozens of large swords. He takes three of these and slings the holders over his shoulder and onto his back. He then quickly turns around and back out of the room. As he steps back into the hallway, the guards catch up to him and point their assault rifles at him.

The captain shouts, "Put down the weapons and get on the ground—now!"

The seraph once again disregards the order and, in the blink of an eye, unsheathes one of the swords, rushes toward the guards, and slaughters every single one of them. Their bodies litter the hallway, and their blood is splattered all over the walls. The seraph quickly runs away, searching for the exit.

Zack slowly awakens to the sound of alarms. Once awake, however, he quickly becomes alert and scans the room. He is no longer in the research wing of the facility but instead in what looks like a security room. There are multiple bodies scattered across the room, and all of the computers in the room have been completely destroyed. He has no idea how or why he came to be here, but he decides that it doesn't matter. After examining the bodies to see if any are alive but finding that none of them are, he quickly exits the room into a large hallway.

He hears gunfire ahead of him in the distance and decides to follow it for reasons he cannot understand. Every instinct he has tells him to run, to get away, but he cannot help but go toward the noise. He has to stop several times to listen for any noise, but after several minutes of running around many different hallways, he discovers that he is close to the source of the sound. Many thoughts run through his head, his heart pounds so hard it feels like it's going to jump out of his body, and his breathing becomes lightning fast. He has no idea what is happening, but he has the burning desire to find out, despite the risk.

Zack turns the next corner to the left and finally discovers the source of the commotion. He stares down a long hallway and, at its center, lies the seraph, standing upright, facing away from him, surrounded by the bloodied corpses of about a dozen guards. Zack's eyes widen, and he lets out a long gasp. The seraph hears this and turns around to face him. Zack sees in the seraph's hand a large sword, the same model he used in the military, with blood dripping off of its blade. The seraph's face is one of extreme malice, and Zack feels like its eyes are staring directly into his soul.

The seraph quickly charges forward, attempting to stab Zack in the gut, but Zack miraculously manages to dodge the attack, as well as the subsequent ones that follow. This confuses both Zack and the seraph, as they both know that he was moving faster than any human could, but the seraph continues to swing at him, and Zack continues to avoid them. Zack then rolls over to one of the bodies, picks up its assault rifle, and begins firing at the seraph, who manages to avoid the shots with relative ease. The seraph then charges toward Zack again, and Zack attempts to block the attack with the rifle, but the sword slices right through it, cutting it in half. Luckily, Zack is able to narrowly avoid the attack before he tries to counterattack by punching the seraph in the face, but it is blocked. The seraph then hits Zack with a hard kick to the stomach, knocking him down to the ground. Just as the seraph attempts to deliver the killing blow, a group of guards come rushing into the hallway and begin firing at the seraph, who manages to skillfully dodge all of the incoming bullets and cut down all of the guards. Zack uses the opportunity to escape and quickly run down another hallway out of sight of the seraph. After taking a few seconds to catch his breath, he begins running toward the exit, cautiously watching out for the seraph the entire time. Thankfully, he doesn't encounter the seraph again and manages to find the exit and get out of the building.

Outside, there is a large crowd of police officers, firefighters, and paramedics. The police have erected a large barrier to hold back the crowd and prevent entry into the building. Many people are being taken inside ambulances and the police have begun entering the building. As soon as Zack walks outside, a group of police officers run up to him and lead him to an ambulance. Inside, he is quickly checked by doctors before being told he is okay and taken out so someone else can be checked.

The situation is complete chaos. Everyone is wondering what happened while the police are restraining people who are trying to enter the building. Even above the noises of the crowd, Zack can still hear gunfire coming from inside the building. He starts to feel a sense of dread; knowing and seeing what the seraph was capable of firsthand, he knows that the guards and the police have no chance of stopping it.

It was…inhumanly fast, he begins to think to himself. *How can anyone stop it? How was I able to fight it? There's no way I could move that fast—how did it not kill me?*

The seraph quickly cuts down another group of guards and continues searching for the way out of the building. He runs down hallway after hallway, eventually finding the exit. Before going outside, he peeks through the door, seeing what's on the other side. He sees a massive crowd of people, along with dozens of vehicles. Then he rushes outside into the sight of the crowd. The police aim their weapons at him and demand he drop the swords. As this is happening, Zack is rushing to the front of the crowd, trying to see what's happening. The seraph swiftly kills all of the police officers, sending the crowd into a panic. People begin rushing away from the seraph, screams filling the air. Zack pushes his way through the crowd until he is in the front.

The seraph immediately sees Zack and quickly attacks Zack, who manages to skillfully avoid all of the seraph's slashes. Zack quickly counterattacks with a hard punch to the seraph's face, stunning him and making him stagger back several feet. However, the seraph quickly recovers and goes back on the offensive. Once again, Zack dodges all the attacks, and eventually a convoy of military vehicles arrives in the scene. Before they can capture or kill the seraph, he quickly runs off. Despite the military searching for days, no trace of him is ever found.

The day after the incident, the military has occupied the facility and the surrounding area in order to conduct an investigation. Many of the people at the facility at the time are taken to a military base for questioning, Zack being among them.

At the facility, a soldier approaches Zack and says, "I need you to come with me."

Zack complies and is lead to a nearby helicopter, where he sits in the back with two other soldiers. One of the soldiers points to a seat, where Zack sits down and puts on the harness attached to it. The seat is extremely uncomfortable, but Zack is used to it by now because he made many flights like this in his time of military service.

The flight lasts about two hours, with very little talking among the soldiers. The wait is torturous for Zack, who hates having to wait with nothing to do. He passes the time by humming songs to himself, but that also gets boring after a while. He then decides to just sit there quietly until the flight is over. After what seems like an eternity, they finally arrive at the base, where Zack takes off his harness, exits the chopper, and is escorted inside.

The place seems very familiar to Zack, although he is not sure why as he knows he has never been here before.

I guess after a while, these places all seem to look the same, Zack thinks to himself.

He is eventually led to an interrogation room, where he sits patiently for a few minutes before a man enters the room with a commanding presence. Zack is startled when he sees the man, as he recognizes him. The man before him is Lieutenant Michael Miller, Zack's commanding officer during his time in the military.

CHAPTER 4

"Hello, Zack," Michael begins casually. "Well, I never expected to see you in one of these places."

Zack replies, "I never expected to be in one of these places either, especially on this end. But what are you doing here?"

"When I heard about the incident and that you were involved, I saw this as a perfect opportunity to see you again. It's been a very long time."

"You came here just to talk to me?"

"Not exactly." Michael places a folder down on the table in front of Zack. Zack hadn't even noticed that he was holding one.

Zack opens the folder, and inside is a series of photos and files detailing every aspect of the seraph. Anything anyone could ever want to know about it is contained inside. Zack quickly looks through and closes the folder.

Afterward, Michael continues, "So do you know what happened?"

Zack answers, "I have no idea."

"Well, tell me what you were doing when it happened."

"Well, it's going to sound a bit…strange."

"Strange how?"

"Well, I was examining the main lab of the facility. I entered the room where the seraph was housed, and I passed out."

"You passed out?"

"Yes. I have no idea what happened. I had a sudden headache that just got worse and worse until I went unconscious. When I woke up, I was in the security room."

"What happened then?"

"Well, everyone in the room was dead. I ran out of the building as fast as I could."

"So do you know where it is now?"

"We lost track of it after it ran off. A lot of people said that you held it off. They called you a hero."

This causes Zack to smirk, then he continues, "I'm not a hero. I just did what I had to."

"Be that as it may, they said that your fighting skills were incredible. They said that you moved unlike anything they had ever seen before."

"I honestly have no idea how I did it."

"Well, I've seen your skills on the battlefield, and I've never seen anything like it, either. You are the greatest soldier I've ever seen."

"Why does it matter? I'm not in the military anymore."

"Well, that's kind of the thing. You see, the military wants you back. I'm asking you to come back."

"You want me to reenlist?"

"Yes. We need you. This country needs you."

"I left the military for a reason. I swore I'd never go back."

"Oh, come on. It wasn't all that bad, was it?"

"No, it wasn't. But I'm still never going back."

"Why not?"

"I swore never to go back after what happened."

"You mean the incident in Marsden?"

"You know damn well that's what I mean. I can never go back after that."

"Zack, you can't blame yourself for what happened there."

"Then who am I supposed to blame? Are you saying that I shouldn't take responsibility for my actions?"

"No, that's not what I am saying. I am simply saying that you shouldn't constantly dwell on something that happened a long time ago."

"I can't go back after that."

"Come on, Zack. That was six years ago."

"But I still remember it like it was yesterday. I think about it every day."

"Zack, won't you please reconsider? We need your help."

"You have millions of soldiers. I'm sure you could take care of the seraph yourself."

"Yes, but not without great cost in lives and resources. With your skills, we could avoid any unnecessary bloodshed."

"*Ha!* When has the government ever cared about how many people they kill?"

"Come on, Zack. You know we're not like that."

"I used to think so. But after the things I saw, I realized that you people don't care about anyone but yourselves."

"If you hate the government so much, why do you still work for them?"

"Because now I don't have a job that involves killing people. And I still need to make a living."

"Listen, Zack. I don't care if you hate me. I don't care if you hate the government. I'm not asking you to do it for them or for me. I'm asking you to do it for the men out there, on the front lines. Putting their lives on the line to protect the people back here at home. Think about how many of them are going to die if you don't help us. You used to call these men brothers, once, or have you forgotten about that?"

Zack lets out a long sigh before responding, "No, I haven't forgotten about that. But I just can't go back out there. I don't want to hurt anyone else."

"Nobody will get hurt, Zack. You will not be in much danger."

"I don't care about that. My own life is unimportant. It's the lives of others that I am afraid of being at risk. I don't want to be responsible for anyone else dying."

"Nobody is going to die."

"How can you be so certain?"

"Because we have a plan, and you are capable."

"And you think I could do this?"

"You didn't seem to have any trouble fighting the seraph back at the facility."

"That was different."

"Different how?"

"It was a tense situation. Hell, it felt like I was barely even in control of my own body."

"Zack, I know your skills and abilities. I know you can do this. I wouldn't even ask you if I didn't think you could."

"So you want me to kill this seraph? By myself?"

"First of all, we don't want you to kill it. We still want to research it. It would be of little use to us dead. Second of all, you won't be alone. We have a special agent assigned to help you should you accept the mission."

"Can I see him?"

"Yes, you can see her."

"A woman?"

"Yeah. I have many highly skilled women under my command."

"I know that. I just wasn't expecting you to send one for this mission. Women usually weren't deployed for these types of assignments."

"A lot has changed since you've left."

"I guess so. In any case, I'd like to meet her."

Michael looks at the guard standing at the door and commands, "Bring her in."

In walks a tall woman with long black hair, tied back into a bun. Zack is surprised when he sees her because she is stunningly beautiful. Her skin is very tan, with an olive-brown color. She is wearing standard military gear, with large tan boots, camouflaged pants, a long-sleeved camouflaged shirt, and a hat. Zack notices several medals attached to her shirt, indicating much combat experience. She slowly saunters in and salutes Michael.

"At ease, Amanda," Michael tells her.

Amanda stops saluting Michael and stands stiffly in front of him.

Michael continues, "Amanda, this is Zack Branford. Zack, this is Amanda Saren."

Amanda swiftly walks over to Michael and holds out her hand, saying, "Pleasure to meet you."

"It's a pleasure to meet you too," Michael says as he shakes her hand.

Michael explains, "Amanda is one of our finest soldiers. She went out on dozens of combat missions during the war against Imperia. She has exemplary skills in combat. She will be a great asset to you in your mission."

Giving Michael a puzzled look, Zack responds, "I haven't even agreed to go on the mission yet."

"Come on, Zack. We could really use your help. You will be paid handsomely for your service."

"I don't care about the money. I don't want to go back out in the line of duty. I'm sorry, Michael, but my answer is no."

Zack sees that Michael is getting visibly frustrated. He responds with, "Zack, I'm not asking you to do this for me. I'm not asking you to do this for the government. I'm asking you to do this for them." He points at the soldier standing by the door. "Do it for all of our hardworking service men and women out there in the field. They are putting their lives on the line each and every day in the service of this country. They have sacrificed so much to protect and serve the people who live here. Do you really want to put them in harm's way more than they have to be? If you don't take this mission, then they will have to, and they will all be putting themselves at risk. Some of them may die during the mission. Now are you really going to let them die just because of your fear? Would you be able to live with yourself afterward, knowing that people died during this mission and that you could've prevented it but refused to?"

After pondering this for several seconds, Zack lets out a long sigh and answers, "No, no I wouldn't. All right, you win. I'll accept the assignment. But this is it. I don't want you or anyone else to ask me this again after this mission is over. You understand?"

Michael responds, "I understand. We will not bother you again once this mission is over. I'm glad you decided to join."

"You didn't leave me much choice. You wouldn't stop asking."

"Well, we really need your help on this mission. I wouldn't be so adamant about it otherwise."

"If you say so. Let's get started."

"All right. Your mission is to track down the seraph and bring him back to us, alive if possible. His body can still be used for research: there is much it can still tell us. You are both going to work together on this."

"Yes, you already told me that."

"Just making sure you know. So, Zack, do you know how the seraph managed to escape?"

"Don't you know? There were guards and security cameras all over the facility."

"Most of the guards in the facility were killed, and all the security footage from the last day has been lost."

"How is that possible?"

"We are not sure at the moment. All of the computers in the security station have been destroyed. Even so, that alone would not be enough to get rid of all of the security footage. We are currently investigating this."

"Well, as I told you, I passed out right when it happened, so I have no idea how he managed to escape."

"All right. Well, is there anything useful you can tell me?"

"Well, he took three swords from the armory."

"Yes, that's what the security team said. All three swords were the same model that you used when you were in the military. But why would he need to steal three swords? Those swords are nearly indestructible, so he wouldn't have to worry about them breaking."

There is silence for several seconds as Amanda, Michael, and Zack ponder this question until Zack figures out the answer.

Zack looks at Michael and says, "I think I know. He stole three swords because there are three seraphs left alive. He wants to free the other seraph."

With wide eyes, Michael replies, "Oh my god. It makes sense. I think you're right. We have to stop him. If he frees the others, they could cause untold amounts of damage."

"How are we supposed to stop him?"

"Well, if he's planning on freeing the other seraph, then he will have to go to the bases where they are held. We know where they all are, so it's just a matter of figuring out which one he will hit first and setting up an ambush there."

"How are we supposed to know which one he will go to first?"

"Well, that's just it, we have no way of knowing."

"Wait, how is he going to know where the other two are? How does he even know there are two others left?"

"Because of the telepathic link the seraph share with each other."

"What the hell are you talking about?"

"We're not really sure how it works, but the seraph are about to communicate with each other telepathically. Meaning they can communicate using nothing but their thoughts."

"I know what telepathy is, thanks. But how do you know this?"

"We conducted tests to study it. We subjected one of the seraph to a great amount of pain, and another seraph reacted to it. He was able to feel the pain that the other seraph was feeling."

"Okay, so how exactly does this telepathic link work? Do they just think something and the other seraph are able to see what they are thinking?"

"We are not sure. We conducted numerous tests on the seraph and scanned their brains extensively. Their brains have all the same parts as a human brain, but there are more. We figured out that some parts allow them to control their enhanced strength and speed, but there is one part of their brain that we still do not fully understand." Michael takes out a picture of a seraph brain and places it in front of Zack. He then points to a place in the upper area of the brain. "This is that area. It has very strange properties, and we do not know what exactly it does. We believe that it controls their telepathic abilities, but there is no way to know for sure."

Zack examines the photograph for a few seconds before responding, "So does this ability of theirs apply to humans as well?"

"No, human brains do not have the same type of brains as them. They can only use their telepathic abilities on each other."

"So this is how he knows where the other seraph are. He's communicating with their minds."

"That's the only theory that makes sense. So now, the question is, which one is he going to go after first?"

"Well, which one is the closest? It would make sense that that would be the one he would try to get to first."

"That would be this one." Michael lays down a picture of a seraph body right in front of Zack.

Zack examines the photo. It shows a female figure with long silver hair. Her body is very muscular, and her skin is pale white. The body is laid across a table, with a piece of cloth covering her breasts and another covering her pubic region. Below the picture, there is a list of statistics about the body, including hair color, eye color, weight, and height. According to this, she is over seven feet tall, weighs over three hundred pounds, and has brown eyes.

When Zack is finished looking at the picture, he looks up to Michael and asks, "So where is she?"

"She is being held in a secret facility in Heren. The country is an ally of ours, so they should be willing to help us. However, we would like to avoid it if possible, as it would cause our country great embarrassment."

"So what's the plan?"

"We are going to send a large military force to the facility, then set up an ambush for seraph and capture it using dozens of high-powered Tasers."

"So what do you need me for, then?"

"You are going to act as bait. We will send you in to lure the seraph into our trap. Once he's in, we will fire all of the Tasers at him, which should incapacitate him."

"Should? You don't even know that this is going to work? If this fails, then dozens could die."

"I know. But there are so many things we still do not understand about the seraph. This is the best plan we have at the moment."

"Don't you think that you should have a Plan B in case this goes wrong?"

"Don't worry, we do have one. If this fails, then we will send in attack helicopters that will incapacitate the seraph without killing him. Don't worry, Zack. You will not be in any danger. We are prepared for a situation like this."

"And what will Amanda's role be in all this?"

"She will provide backup for you in case you need it. If the plan goes awry, she can help get you out of there safely."

"All right. When do we move out?"

"We will first have to get our forces established at the base. We should be ready in about two days."

"Okay, what am I going to do until then?"

"We will provide you with a room to stay in, as well as access to our training area. Use them as you wish."

"All right," Zack replies. Michael then begins exiting the room, but just as he opens the door, Zack says, "Michael..."

Michael turns around and asks, "Yes, Zack?"

Zack answers, "It's good to see you again."

"You too," Michael responds.

CHAPTER 5

MICHAEL EXITS THE room, with Zack and Amanda right behind him.

Zack quickly walks to the training room. Inside, he sees a myriad of workout equipment, a shooting range, a wrestling mat, and a sword training area. He goes to the shooting range, and he is greeted by an instructor inside.

"Welcome to the shooting range," the instructor says as Zack is closing the door to the range behind him.

"Hello," Zack replies.

The instructor briefly looks at Zack and asks, "Are you Zack Branford?"

With a puzzled look, Zack asks, "I'm sorry, do I know you?"

The instructor answers, "No, but I was told of your arrival on the base by Lieutenant Miller. I've been told to provide you with whatever you need."

Zack replies, "Well, I would like to try out one of your handguns, if that's all right."

"Which kind would you like?"

"I would like a Desert Fox, if possible."

"Are you sure? You know, those things have one hell of a kick to them."

After thinking it over for a second, Zack answers, "You know what? You're right. I'll take a Mark 21 instead."

"Please, wait here." The instructor leaves for about a minute before returning with the weapon Zack asked for, along with several magazines. He then says to Zack, "Now I need to tell you about how this weapon works before you can use it."

Zack responds, "Don't worry. I am already familiar with how to use it."

"Maybe so, but I've still got to give you the full instructions. It's a matter of safety, you understand."

"Yes, I understand."

Zack listens to the instructor explain how to use the weapon for several minutes, after which, the instructor points Zack to a nearby open lane and tells him, "You can find your goggles and hearing protection over there. I'll be watching you from here."

"Thank you, sir."

"Good shooting."

"Thanks."

The instructor returns to his desk as Zack walks over to the lane and puts on his goggles and ear protection and loads the first magazine into the pistol. He then clicks the safety off and aims at the paper target at the end of the lane. With shaky hands, he begins firing at the target. He goes through the whole magazine in about a minute. After ejecting the magazine, he looks at the target, and is surprised to see that all of his shots hit the center of the target.

I guess I've still got it, Zack thinks to himself. He decides to stop firing and gives the equipment back to the instructor.

After exiting the firing range, Zack decides to work out at the gym. When he arrives, he sees Amanda running on one of the dozens of treadmills. Zack walks to the rack of weights and begins lifting the dumbbells. After easily lifting the 100-pound weights, he picks up two 200-pound weights, which he also lifts with ease. He then picks up two 500-pound dumbbells, and like the others, he is able to lift them easily.

Amanda starts watching Zack, amazed at his strength. She turns off the treadmill and walks over to him, saying, "Wow, I never knew how strong you were!"

Zack replies, "Well, you kind of have to be to be in the military."

"Yeah, but you haven't been in the military for a long time, have you?"

"I've kept up with my training regiment, even after I quit," Zack lied. He hadn't worked out ever since he left the military. He was just as surprised about his strength as she was.

"Yeah…look, I have to go. See you later."

"Bye," Zack says as Amanda leaves the gym. He then decides that he had also had enough working out, so he put the weights back on the rack and leaves the gym. Feeling tired, he walks to his room, which is down a large hallway. Once he opens the door, he takes a quick look around the small room.

There is a large bed against the left wall, a footlocker along the back right wall, a closet against the back wall, and a dresser along the right wall. The walls and ceiling are painted a dull gray color, while the floor has brown carpeting.

Zack takes a look inside the footlocker and finds nothing inside. He does the same with the dresser, but that is empty as well. Zack then realizes that he left the door open, so he quickly walks to the entrance to the room and quietly closes the door behind him. The door has the same gray color as the walls and ceiling.

Feeling tired, Zack decides to go to sleep, even though it's very early. He looks at his phone and sees that it is only 9:37 p.m., he usually goes to sleep around 2:00 or 3:00 in the morning because he has trouble sleeping unless it is very late at night. However, Zack is exhausted, so he turns his phone off, puts it on top of the dresser, and lies down on the bed. It has a very flat, uncomfortable mattress, just like it was during his days in the military.

Despite his exhaustion, Zack still has trouble getting to sleep. He tosses and turns in his bed for hours, constantly thinking about the events of the past day. He is unable to stop thinking about his battle with the seraph. All of the fear, the adrenaline, the exertion, the inhumanly fast speed with which it moved—these images stuck in Zack's mind with vivid detail. Finally, after about three hours of lying in bed awake, he manages to slowly drift off to sleep.

CHAPTER 6

MILLER ENTERS ZACK'S room and finds him lying face up on the bed with a somewhat pained expression on his face. He walks to the bed and gives Zack a push on his shoulder. Zack wakes up suddenly and immediately sits up in his bed.

"Bad dream?" Michael asks as Zack looks at him.

Zack gives the simple response, "Yeah."

"Well, get up. You have training to do."

"Yeah, yeah," Zack moans as he gets out of bed and starts to change his clothing.

As he is leaving, Michael tells Zack, "You should speak with Amanda. She's in the gym now."

"All right," Zack says as he finishes getting dressed. He leaves the room right after Michael and heads to the gym. When he arrives, he sees Amanda doing pull-ups in the center of the gym. She has her hair tied up in a bun, and she is wearing black shorts and a white muscle shirt. Zack notices that she has incredibly muscular arms and legs, and he also sees sweat dripping down the back of her neck, suggesting that she has been working out for a while already.

Zack calls out, "Well, someone's been working hard this morning."

Amanda gets off the bar and sees Zack, replying, "Well, look who finally decided to show up. Have a nice sleep, did we?"

"Yeah," Zack lied, "I thought I'd let you get a head start."

"You really think I need one?"

"No, I guess not."

"Exactly. I can hold my own just like anyone else here."

"Yeah, I noticed."

Amanda resumes her pull-ups as Zack gets on a nearby tread-mill and begins to run. While he does this, Amanda resumes the conversation, asking, "So how long were you in the service?"

Zack looks at her with a puzzled look, and after thinking about it for a few seconds, he responds, "About five years," he answers. "Why do you ask?"

"I just want to know you a little, since we're going to be going out on a mission together."

"I guess that's fair. What about you? How long have you been in the service?"

"Almost four years now." She pauses for a few seconds before asking, "So why'd you quit? The way Miller talked about you, it sounds like you were great at it. You could have been an officer by now."

"I'd rather not talk about it."

"Okay, whatever you say," she says before stopping her pull-ups and walking out of the gym.

Zack is then left to work out alone until lunch. They serve him spaghetti and toast and he has a glass of milk with it.

He sifts his way through the tables and the dozens of other military officials eating and talking to each other. Eventually, he manages to find an empty table in the back corner of the mess hall, and he sits here and eats his lunch by himself. About a minute later, Miller enters the hall and gets his lunch. Scanning the room for a few seconds, he eventually sees where Zack is sitting a makes his way there. He sits across from Zack and asks, "So how do you like the facility?"

Looking up from his lunch, Zack sees that Miller is sitting with him, not even noticing him until now. He then answers with, "It's pretty nice. You must have done pretty well for yourself after I left to be stationed at a place like this."

"Yeah, I suppose you could say that. Although things have gotten much quieter since the war ended."

"I bet. What have you been doing since then?"

"You know I'm not allowed to tell you that. I'd have to kill you if I did."

Zack rolls his eyes at the commander's stupid joke, then continues eating. Before he can finish, Michael asks, "So are you ready for your mission?"

"You know," Zack begins, "you really didn't give me much time to prepare."

"I know, but we can't afford to wait. That thing is out in the wild, and if we are correct, trying to free all the other test subjects. If that happens, then many innocent people could die. That's why we have to hurry."

"You don't need to tell me about the danger that those things pose. I witnessed it firsthand. Besides, I was just being facetious about you not giving me time to train. I'm well aware that time is of the essence."

"Yes, well, you never actually answered my question. You will be deploying tomorrow, and I want to make sure that you are ready."

"I'm as ready as I possibly can be under the circumstances."

"We'll just have to hope that that's enough. But don't worry, you will be given plenty of support from a dozen of the best soldiers this country has to offer. You won't be in very much danger."

"Well, that's good to know."

"Hey, Zack, when you're finished eating, I want you to come to the armory so that we can show you the gear you will be given for this mission."

"All right," Zack says as he finishes his meal. He then disposes of all his trash and returns his tray.

As instructed, he makes his way to the armory, where a soldier is standing in front of the door. Zack walks up to the soldier and introduces himself.

"Hello, my name is Zack Branford. Lieutenant Miller told me to meet him here."

The soldier replies, "Yes, he told me that you were coming. Wait here for a moment." He then unlocks and opens the door behind him and motions for Zack to enter.

Zack walks through the door, where he finds a large assortment of weapons, armor, and all of the other equipment that a soldier could possibly need.

The soldier turns to Zack and says, "The lieutenant is here to see you."

Zack turns to face the entrance to see Miller sauntering toward him. When he enters, he says, "Hello again, Zack. I'm glad to see you got here in a timely fashion." Wasting no time, Miller makes his way to the wall to Zack's right and picks up a piece of armor and a helmet, before telling Zack, "This is what you will be wearing on your mission." As he hands them to Zack, he continues, "These are standard issue pieces of armor given to soldiers in the field. The suit is made out of celendra (a flexible material similar to Kevlar) and is designed to withstand the force of a bullet and protect against explosive weapons and blades."

As Miller is explaining, Zack begins to put on the armor and helmet.

Miller continues his explanation, "And the helmet is made of ashela (a lightweight metal) and will protect your head from shrapnel and blunt force trauma."

Just as Miller is finishing his explanation, Zack finishes putting on the equipment, after which he says, "It feels a bit different than the equipment I wore years ago."

Miller replies, "That's because the design has been updated a bit since you left. This new equipment has been designed to be more lightweight to allow for better mobility without giving up any of its effectiveness."

"Yeah, it does feel a bit more comfortable, but it still feels kind of awkward."

"Yes, well, this stuff is designed for function, not comfort. I'm sure you'll adjust to it in no time."

"Yeah, I grew accustomed to wearing this kind of stuff."

"Glad to hear it," Miller responds as he takes a pair of guns off the wall before continuing. "These will be your primary weapons for this mission." As he hands one of them to Zack, he explains, "This is a T800 Taser. It is capable of delivering a non-lethal electric shock to a target up to thirty feet away. A shock can also be emitted directly from the tip of the weapon without needing it to be fired."

As Zack is examining the weapon, he says, "I've never used one of these before."

"Don't worry. Compared to real guns, these are simple to use. You shouldn't have any trouble." Miller then hands the other gun to Zack and explains, "This is a Cobra Dart weapon. It fires tranquilizer darts up to fifty feet. This will be your backup weapon for your mission. It should be enough to put the target to sleep in a matter of seconds."

Zack examines the new weapon for several seconds before asking Miller, "Is there anything else I will need?"

Miller takes a knife off the wall and answers, "Yes, you will also be given a tactical knife just like this one. You shouldn't need to use it, but you will still want to take it just in case." He briefly shows the knife to Zack before placing it back in its place.

Zack gives the weapons back to Miller and takes off the armor to return to him as well. Miller places all the equipment back in their proper place before telling Zack, "You will be briefed on your mission at 1800. Try to get some training in until then."

Zack responds with, "Yes, sir."

"You don't need to call me sir, Zack."

"Oh, really? I thought that's what all soldiers had to say to their commanding officers."

"You're not a soldier anymore. Plus we're friends. You don't need to be so formal around me."

"All right. If you say so. Is there anything else you would like to tell me?"

"No, that will be all for now. You are dismissed."

"I guess I'll be seeing you at 1800 then."

Miller and Zack leave the armory together, and Zack goes to the shooting range to practice with the weapons he will be using on the mission. Miller goes a separate way; where he's going Zack doesn't know.

When he reaches the shooting range, Zack sees the instructor once again standing right behind the door, waiting to greet anyone who comes through. As he enters, the instructor welcomes him once again. "Well, look who's back. Come to do some more shooting?"

Zack answers, "Yes, sir."

"Well, what will you be using this time?"

"I'd like a T800 Taser and a Cobra Dart weapon, please."

"As you wish. Wait here." The instructor leaves to get the equipment and returns with it about two minutes later. "Here you go," the instructor says as he hands the equipment to Zack. "Now, as before, I need to teach you how to use these weapons before you are allowed to use them."

Zack replies, "All right."

The instructor spends several minutes explaining how to fire and reload the weapons. After his explanation, he tells Zack, "Lane 18 is open. You may use it."

"Thank you," Zack responds as he takes the weapons, ammunition, goggles, and hearing protection. He gets everything ready as he walks to his lane. When he gets there, he begins by practicing with the Taser. He manages to hit the target right in the center of the body. He quickly reloads the weapon and fires it again, and once again, he is able to hit the target straight in the center. He then puts down the Taser and picks up the Cobra, loads a dart into the barrel, and takes aim at the target, putting the dart straight into the center. He reloads the gun and fires again; once again, hitting the target straight in the middle. Satisfied with his performance, he takes all his equipment back to the instructor.

As Zack hands the equipment to him, the instructor gives Zack a confused expression and asks, "Are you done already?"

Zack answers, "Yes, sir."

"Well, that was fast. Are you sure you don't want to put in some more practice?"

"No, I'm fine, thank you."

"See you later." The instructor returns the equipment to their proper places as Zack leaves the shooting range.

Zack then decides to return to the gym to exercise. He runs on a treadmill for about half an hour before deciding that he's had enough. Looking at the clock, he sees that it says 1354, meaning that he still has an hour until dinner, and another four hours after that until briefing. Deciding that he's had enough training, he returns to his room to wait out the remaining time. When he gets inside his room and gently closes the door behind himself, he lays on his bed and starts to think about his encounter with the seraph. His memories come rushing back to him—the intensity, the rush of adrenaline, his heart beating a mile a minute, the feeling of helplessness as he faces down a menacing foe with nothing to protect himself. Then there was the speed. The speed with which it moved, so fast one could barely see it, like it was a bullet that had just been fired from a gun. Yet somehow, Zack was able to avoid its attacks, and even get in an attack of his own. He couldn't explain it, not even to himself. It was like his instincts had taken over, and he was no longer in control of his own body, like it was moving all by itself. He remembers the expression on its face, a look of pure hatred, the look of a single-minded entity whose purpose was the death of everything around it. The look terrified Zack, made him wonder what had been done to the poor creature to fill it with such malice. All of these horrific memories and emotions came rushing back to Zack like a tidal wave.

Suddenly, Zack snaps back into reality. He quickly sits up in his bed, panting rapidly and sweating profusely. He looks at the clock next to his bed, which reads 1502. Realizing that it is now dinnertime, he quickly showers and changes his clothes. He then rushes to the mess hall, where they are serving pork chops.

Zack gets his meal and sits down at the same spot he sat at lunch. He is still breathing quickly because of his dream, though he doesn't know why. He has faced many life-threatening situations before, but for some reason, his encounter with the seraph scared him unlike any other.

Come on, get a hold of yourself, Zack thinks to himself. *It was just one person—you've been up against much greater odds before.*

As he begins eating, he notices his hands are shaking, so much so that he can barely hold his fork. He puts his fork down and hides his hands underneath the table, trying desperately to calm himself down.

Suddenly, Zack notices Amanda walking toward him, and he forces himself to slow his breathing, hoping she won't notice his nervousness.

"Hello, Zack," Amanda greets him. "How are you doing?"

Zack answers, "I'm fine. How about you?"

"Oh, I'm doing fine myself."

"That's good to hear."

There was an awkward silence between the two before Amanda asks, "So how do you like this place?"

"It's really nice. Much nicer than any of the places I lived in during my time in the service."

"Yeah, this place was built not too long ago. It's probably the nicest military facility in the entire country."

"Interesting. So how did you get lucky enough to be stationed here?"

"I've had great success in my career. Eventually, the higher-ups discovered my talents and gave me a job here."

"So what, this is where you live whenever you're not out on a mission?"

"Yeah."

"How long have you been here?"

"About a year now. This place has become like a home to me."

"And what about your real home? Where do you live?"

"I live here."

"I mean, where do you live when you're on leave?"

"I live in Arcturus."

"Really? Is it nice there?"

"Yeah."

"Does your family live there too?"

"I'd rather not talk about that."

"O...kay," Zack replies questioningly. However, he doesn't push the issue, figuring she must have her reasons. He then asks, "So what made you want to join the military anyway?"

Amanda answers, "It...just seemed like a good job. What about you? What made you want to join?"

Zack suspected she was hiding something, but he couldn't quite put his finger on it. He also didn't want to pry, so instead he answers, "Well, I don't want to sound like I'm bragging, but I have always been rather gifted, physically and intellectually. I figured that the military would be the perfect place to put my talents to use."

"Well, I already knew about your physical prowess."

Zack starts to blush a little when Amanda says this.

"So what, you just did really well in school and figured you could hack it here as well?"

"Pretty much, yeah."

"Well, from what the lieutenant has told me, you would be right. He holds you in pretty high regard."

"Well, we're good friends. Of course he thinks highly of me."

"No, this goes beyond mere friendship. He says that you were the greatest soldier he's ever seen."

"I wouldn't go that far. I wasn't that great."

"Well, that's just what he says."

"Yeah, well, I think Miller has kind of exaggerated some of his stories a bit. I was really nothing special."

"I don't know. I mean, you survived an encounter with one of those seraph things. That's pretty extraordinary. Those things are fierce and tough."

"I was just doing what was necessary to survive."

"Yeah, but that goes beyond just survival instinct. I mean, I've studied them and know a lot about them. No ordinary person could possibly survive something like that. I honestly have no idea how you did it."

"I just got lucky, I guess."

"Well, that was one hell of a lucky break then."

"I guess so," Zack plainly responds before turning his attention to his meal. He doesn't want to let Amanda know exactly what happened, as he didn't think she would believe him. He hardly believes it himself. He shouldn't have been able to move as fast as he did; no human could have.

After finishing his meal, Zack quickly gets up, throws away his trash, and leaves, not wanting to talk about the incident any further.

Upon returning to his room, he looks at the clock next to his bed, which says 1541. He then lays down on his bed and gets lost in his thoughts. He continues playing the battle over and over again in his mind, remembering every detail vividly. Suddenly, the alarm on Zack's clock goes off. Snapping back to reality once again he quickly turns the alarm on the clock off. It says 1750, meaning that the mission briefing will begin in ten minutes. Zack quickly puts on a new set of clothing and heads down to the briefing room, eager to learn his role in the upcoming operation.

CHAPTER 7

Zack arrives at the briefing room at 1758, and the room is already filled with personnel, most of whom Zack doesn't recognize. Miller is standing at the front of the room, standing beside a projector screen along the wall behind him, which is blank. Zack sits on the far side of the room by himself, not wanting to talk to Amanda after their conversation at dinner. As soon as 1800 strikes, the door to the room is closed and locked, ensuring nobody else can walk in.

Miller then begins speaking, "Hello, everyone, my name is Lieutenant Michael Miller, as all of you are aware, and I will be the commanding officer for this mission." The screen behind Miller flips to show a picture of the seraph that escaped from the base as Miller continues speaking. "Approximately thirty minutes ago, our satellites took this picture of the fugitive seraph just outside of Aranea, Moorson. Now as some of you may know,"—the screen flips to a picture of a large government base—"this city is home to a facility owned and operated by the Moorson government. It is called the Aranea Institute of Research, and inside"—the screen once again flips to a new picture, this one showing another seraph—"is another captive seraph."

The seraph on the screen was female, with long, golden hair, who looked like she was in her early twenties and was extremely beautiful. She was kept in a large storage pod, unconscious, and was completely naked except for two cloths covering her breasts and vaginal area.

Miller continues, "We believe that the seraph that escaped is attempting to find and rescue the one in this facility. We are unsure how it found out about the location of this facility or the seraph it houses, but we believe that it has to do with the psychic link that all seraph have. We must capture the seraph before it reaches the facility, where it could harm some of the personnel there." The screen behind Miller flips to a picture of a map, with the city appearing on the top edge and numerous lines drawn all over it, and the facility on the bottom right edge.

Miller continues, "So here is the plan. At 0600, Alpha team, led by Amanda, will drop Zack off right here." Miller points to a position on the map then resumes. "Alpha team will then drop here." Miller points to another position on the map. "Zack will then lure out the seraph, at which point Bravo Team will arrive from here"— Miller points to another position on the map—"armed with Tasers. Alpha team will then come out of their positions and join bravo team at Zack's position. Then, when both teams are in position, they fire all fire on the fugitive seraph at once. We must make sure to keep the seraph away from the facility in order to protect the people there. Whatever happens, the seraph *must not* be allowed inside the facility. I cannot specify this enough. Now the plan is simple, and this operation should not be difficult or take long. We have to wrap this up quickly before anyone realizes what has happened, as this will cause great national embarrassment. Now are there any questions?"

The room is silent for several seconds. Then Miller finishes, "All right then, everyone get some rest. You all have a big day tomorrow."

Everyone in the room gets up to leave as the guard at the door unlocks it to let everyone out.

As everyone is walking out of the room, Miller walks over to Zack and asks, "Are you all right, Zack?"

Zack answers, "Yeah, I guess so."

"Are you sure? This could be very dangerous."

"I'm fine, really. You said it yourself, this mission is going to be short and simple. I'm sure everything will be fine."

"I admire your optimism. Just use those skills that you've built over the years and you'll be just fine."

"Thanks a lot. Is there anything else?"

"No. I just wanted to see how you were feeling."

"Well, don't worry. I'm feeling fine."

"I'm glad to hear that. Go get ready for tomorrow."

"I will. Thanks for the pep talk." Zack stands up and looks at the clock, which says 1815. He then leaves the room, which is mostly empty by now as almost everyone has already left. Zack, Miller, and the guard at the door are the only people left in the room.

Upon exiting, the guard at the door says to Zack, "Have a nice day."

Zack replies simply with, "You too," then leaves the room. The hallway is filled with the hustle and bustle of people walking to and fro, many of them in conversation with each other, and some just standing around and talking to each other. Zack leaves the hallway and heads back to his room.

He doesn't know what to do now, having several hours of free time to do whatever he wants. The briefing ended up being much shorter than Zack had anticipated, as he was used to them lasting at least an hour. He didn't want to work out or go to the shooting range, as he felt there was no point in either activity because he has already mastered them both. However, he also doesn't want to go to sleep, not that he could even if he wanted to with the constant thoughts of battle and death stuck in his mind. So he decides to simply walk to a nearby balcony hanging outside the building and see the view.

From here, he sees a nearby forest, and in the distance, he could see a nearby city. It is full of activity, with cars driving every which way, to people walking on the sidewalks, to the buildings, which were beautifully illuminated against the evening darkness. Meanwhile, the forest is almost completely still, as there are very few animals in the area. The trees are almost all full of lush, dark green leaves, covering thick, brown trunks. The view is absolutely gorgeous, and Zack tries to memorize every detail he could so that maybe he would have something to think about tonight to keep him calm and help him sleep. It is pretty quiet from where Zack is standing, which he likes, as it helps bring him some measure of peace, even if it is only for a short time. He stands there for a very long time, admiring the view, until he eventually goes inside to escape from the autumn chill.

When he arrives back inside, he immediately looks for the nearest clock, which says 2034. The hallway is mostly empty, as most of the personnel are in the cafeteria for the final meal of the day. Zack quickly walks there so that he could have something to eat before going to bed.

When he arrives, the cafeteria is full of people, most of whom are already seated and eating or talking. He enters the nearest line and gets his meal, which is chicken noodle soup with saltine crackers, a banana, a small slice of chocolate cake, and milk. Due to the line being empty, Zack is able to get through and get his food in only about a minute. The chef hands Zack his meal and says in a friendly tone, "Enjoy your meal."

He takes his food and sits in the nearest empty seat. This time, there is nobody around that Zack knows, thus he is able to eat without interruption. He quietly eats his entire meal, throws away his trash, and then leaves the cafeteria.

He then decides to visit the recreation room, which has a television with a huge screen. Taking the remote, Zack flips through the channels until he finds his favorite show, *Paranormal Hunters*. The show is about a family that investigates crimes that are perpetrated by monsters, usually murders. The family is comprised of a mother, a father, and two children; the oldest is a fifteen-year-old boy while the youngest is a thirteen-year-old girl. The monsters they hunt range from vampires, werewolves, and zombies to ghosts, demons, and angels, and many other types of monsters as well. The show is, of course, completely fictional, as it takes place in an alternate world where all these things actually exist. The current episode shows the family hunting a strigoi, a monster from Romanian folklore that are corpses risen from their graves in order to drink the blood of the living, similar to vampires. The episode is already more than halfway over, but Zack doesn't care, as he has already seen the episode about half a dozen times. He sits back and watches the rest of the episode until the time 2100 rolls around, when the episode is over. At that point, several other people have walked into the room, and Zack leaves and heads back to his own room. Once inside, Zack takes off all his clothing except for his underwear, lays in his bed, and pulls the blanket over his body up to his shoulders. He then tries desperately to fall asleep, but to no avail. Thoughts of the battle against the seraph, as well as the upcoming mission tomorrow keep his mind busy all night and keep him awake. He quietly lies in his bed for seventeen torturous hours until finally, at last, the alarm on his clock rings 0600, time for Zack to prepare for his mission.

CHAPTER 8

Zack quickly rises out of bed, takes a quick shower, changes clothes, and heads to the briefing room. When he gets there, the room is teeming with people, just like last night.

After waiting for about five minutes, Miller addresses the room, "All right everyone. The mission is a go, and it is time for all of you to suit up. Everyone, to the armory."

Miller then leads everyone in the room to the armory. There, everyone puts on their combat outfits and grabs all the necessary gear and supplies. Zack puts on his armor quickly before heading over to the wall of guns to pick up his weapons.

Amanda is already there when Zack gets there, and when he arrives, she greets him with, "Hey, so are you ready for this?"

Zack answers, "As ready as I'll ever be. How about you?"

"I think so."

"That's good to know."

"You look nervous."

"Well, I guess I kind of am."

"Don't worry about it. Everyone gets nervous right before a mission. I am as well—I've just gotten good at hiding it."

Zack smiles slightly before replying, "Thanks. That really helps."

"Don't mention it."

Miller comes up behind them and interrupts, "Knock off the chit-chat. You need to be gearing up."

Zack and Amanda both quickly grab all their gear and put it in the proper places without any more talking.

As soon as every team member is fully geared up, Miller announces, "Follow me to the helipad." Miller leads everyone to the helipad, where all the team members board a helicopter prepared for the mission. The helicopter has already started running before they get there, letting out a deafening noise. Once everyone is on board, Miller yells, "All right everyone, good luck!" before stepping back and letting the helicopter ascend. Miller stands and watches as the helicopter leaves then returns inside the base.

During the ride to the mission, several of the team members talk to each other about various things that Zack doesn't pay attention to. He sits quietly in his seat for the entire ride, not feeling like talking to anyone.

After several hours, the helicopter finally arrives at its destination, the outskirts of Aranea. After getting into position, the helicopter pilot radios to the teams, "All right, we are clear for drop. Everyone, exit the chopper."

Two team members drop the ropes on both sides of the helicopter, then everyone quickly rappels down. Everyone makes it on the ground safely, then the helicopter flies away to the designated area.

Now on the ground, everyone moves to their designated position, while Zack stands out in the open, waiting for the seraph to arrive. He unsheathes his sword and scans his surroundings, looking for any sign of movement or any other sign of the seraph's position.

Nothing happens for several minutes until suddenly, Zack starts having a searing headache. He holds his head in his hands and lets out a low, pained growl and collapses to his knees.

As this is happening, Amanda calls Zack on the radio. "Zack, what's going on?"

Zack tries to concentrate through the pain but to no avail. Suddenly, out of the corner of his eye, Zack notices something in the distance; there is movement in the brush. The seraph then emerges, wearing a pair of leather pants and a plain black T-shirt and still brandishing the sword he stole.

The headache subsides, and Zack prepares for battle. The seraph charges him quickly and swings his sword, but Zack is able to narrowly block the strike with his blade.

Alpha and Bravo teams both emerge from their hiding places, their weapons ready to fire. The seraph takes its attention off Zack in order to focus on the rest of the soldiers. Just as fast as the first time, the seraph cuts its way through both teams, slaughtering all of them. However, before it is able to kill Amanda, Zack uses his sword to block the blow. Undeterred, the seraph punches Zack straight in the gut before knocking Amanda out with a blow to her head. Reeling from the force of the blow, Zack is unable to stop the seraph from running into the nearby facility.

As soon as he gets his faculties back, Zack rushes into the facility, intent on stopping the seraph and saving everyone inside. However, when he gets to the entrance, he finds the corpses of guards and scientists strewn about the place, and blood splatters all over the ground. This doesn't stop Zack, as he rushes inside, still wanting to save as many people as he can. Zack is able to get inside thanks to the security system being completely shut down.

Inside, Zack finds even more bodies and blood splattered everywhere. He rushes forward in search of the seraph and, after running down several hallways, finally finds it. However, it is not alone, as accompanying it is the blond seraph, now wielding another sword. As soon as the brown-haired seraph catches sight of Zack, it rushes toward him once again. Zack and the seraph fight each other bitterly as the other seraph escapes. After several minutes of fighting, the seraph tries to escape. Zack takes out his Taser and shoots the seraph in the back with it. The seraph briefly pauses then tears the hooks out of its back and continues running.

Zack chases after it, not wanting to let it get away. However, the seraph is far too fast for Zack to be able to catch up to him, and Zack loses the seraph quickly. He searches the facility for several minutes but eventually gives up.

He then runs out of the facility, and outside, it is surrounded by soldiers and other military personnel. One of the soldiers notices

Zack and rushes up to him, leading him to a nearby doctor to be examined. After the examination, Zack is taken to a nearby chopper and flown back to base.

CHAPTER 9

As ZACK ARRIVES back at the base, Miller stands waiting on the helipad, with a stone-hard expression on his face. Once the helicopter lands, Miller immediately walks up and tells Zack, "Follow me." Miller leads Zack to the briefing room to debrief Zack on the mission.

Miller begins with, "What the hell happened out there?"

Zack answers, "The seraph. It moves so fast. It's impossible to catch."

"This was supposed to be a quick and simple mission and you blew it, hard. Now the whole world knows that we can't keep a single fugitive contained. Do you have any idea what this will do to our country's reputation?"

"The country's reputation? Is that all you care about? What about the people that died back there? And what about their families?"

"You are the one that let those people die in the first place!"

"I did all that I could! You have no idea what these things are capable of!"

"I know damn well what these things are capable of! That's why I sent my best units to capture it!"

"Why do we have to capture it alive? Why can't we just kill it? Clearly, these things are far too dangerous for us to handle!"

"You should have been able to handle it just fine! I gave you more than enough men to do it!"

"Clearly, you didn't, and now they're all dead because you are more concerned with this country's image than protecting people!"

"I do care about protecting people! And for your information, they're not all dead!"

"What? Who survived?"

"Amanda. She's in the infirmary right now, but her injuries are not life-threatening."

"I need to see her right now."

"You will do no such thing! You are getting put on a chopper and being sent home tomorrow. Your involvement in this mission is over."

"Like hell it is! I'm not leaving. I've now survived two encounters with these things, which is more than anyone else can say. I'm not going until the job is done."

Miller pauses for a moment before continuing, "Look, this isn't my decision. These orders are coming straight from the brass. If it were up to me, you would stay on mission, but it's not. I'm sorry."

"Let me talk to them. I know I can convince them to let me stay."

"I can call in a few favors and get you an audience with the council, but I make no guarantees that they will listen to you. Now go, go see Amanda. She's been wanting to talk to you anyway."

"Thank you. I'll find a way to convince them. I swear it."

"You better, or you'll owe me big."

After their conversation, Zack rushes down to the infirmary to see Amanda. One of the staff members directs him to her room, and Zack navigates the halls of the infirmary, walking past several doctors and patients along the way, until he finally reaches it.

Inside, Zack finds Amanda lying on her bed with bandages wrapped around the top of her head. He gently knocks on the open door to let her know that he has arrived.

Amanda quickly turns her head to see Zack standing in the doorway and exclaims, "Zack! Thank you for coming."

Zack responds with, "Of course I came. Once I found out you were here, I just had to come and see you."

"Well, I'm really glad that you're here. I wanted to thank you for what you did back there."

"What do you mean?"

"You saved my life! Of course I had to thank you for that."

"I only did what anybody would have done in the situation. There is really no need to thank me."

"Of course there is. Saving a person's life is a big deal."

"But I couldn't save any of the others. Everyone else is dead because of me."

"Hey, don't blame yourself. You did everything you could given the situation. Just be glad that the two of us are still here."

"I can't. I let all those men and their families down. Now there are twelve families without husbands and fathers. How can I be glad about that?"

"Because you did your best. None of us could have known what would happen. In our line of work, death is always a possibility. Those men, they knew what they signed up for. They wouldn't want you beating yourself up either."

Zack takes a deep breath then responds, "You're right. I'm sorry. I let my emotions get the best of me."

"It's okay, Zack. It happens to everyone."

"Thanks for the reassurance. By the way, how are you feeling? You look like you took a pretty bad blow to the head there."

"I'm fine, trust me. It looks worse than it is."

"Are you sure you're okay?"

"I'm positive. You don't need to worry about me."

"Well, that's a relief. Do you know how long you're going to be in here?"

"A couple days, at most. Like I said, it's really not that bad."

"Do you have a concussion?"

"Just a mild one."

"That's a relief. So other than that, how are you feeling?"

"Not well. I knew many of the men on that mission. Some of us were good friends."

"I'm sorry. You must miss them dearly."

"Yeah, I do."

"So what are you going to do now?"

"What do you mean?"

"I mean, are you going to stay?"

"Of course I am. Sure, I'll miss my friends, but they would want me to keep going. I have to stay, for their sake."

"These sound like some really good men."

"They were, all of them. They were some of the best men I have ever known."

"I bet they were. I'm so sorry that I couldn't save them."

"Zack, I already told you not to beat yourself up over this. You did everything you could. There is no shame in that."

"Try telling that to the higher-ups."

"What are you talking about?"

"They want to send me home and get someone else to do the job."

"What? That's terrible. You are the best person for the mission."

"I think so too, which is why I'm going to convince them to let me stay."

"What? How are you even going to talk to them?"

"Miller said that he can call in some favors to get me an audience with them."

"How are you going to convince them to let you stay?"

"I don't know yet. But I will find a way."

"I'm rooting for you, Zack."

"Thanks. Is there anything else you wanted?"

"No, I don't think so."

"I'm going to head out then. I hope you get better soon."

"Thanks. I hope you get to stay longer."

"I hope so too, bye." Zack leaves the infirmary and goes back to his room. He begins practicing his speech to the council, trying out different lines and deliveries in an attempt to convince them to let him stay. After about an hour of this, there is a knock on Zack's door.

When he answers it, a soldier on the other side says, "Lieutenant Miller would like to speak with you. He's in his office."

Zack replies, "I'm not sure where that is, could you lead me there?"

"Of course, sir. Just follow me," the soldier answers as Zack steps out of his room and closes the door behind him.

The soldier leads Zack down a series of hallways until they come to a beige door with a sign on the wall next to it saying "Office of Lieutenant Michael Miller." The soldier knocks twice on the door, which is followed by, "Come in," from inside the room. The soldier opens the door for Zack, who quickly steps inside to see Miller sitting at his desk typing on his computer.

As Zack walks in, Miller looks up from his computer and greets Zack with, "Hello, Zack. Please sit down." Miller points to the chair sitting in front of the desk, and Zack promptly sits down in it. Miller continues, "I have arranged for you a meeting with the Council of Military Affairs tomorrow at 7:00 a.m. There, you will plead your case to be kept on mission."

Zack responds, "Thank you very much. Don't worry, I will convince them to let me stay. I promise."

"I hope so. I too think that you are the best man for this mission. Let's just hope you can get the council to see it."

"Is there anything else you wanted?"

"No. Now if you'll excuse me, I have much work to do."

"Thanks again," Zack says as he leaves Miller's office. He then returns to his room and continues practicing his speech to the council until 9:00, where he takes a shower and goes to bed.

CHAPTER 10

At 6:00 A.M., Zack wakes up and immediately takes a shower, changes into nice clothes (Miller left some for him), and begins practicing his speech to the council. This goes on until 6:50, at which point a knock comes on Zack's door. He answers, and there is a soldier on the other side, who says, "Good morning, sir. I am here to take you to the council chambers."

Zack follows the soldier to the council chamber, where there is a set of double doors, with several chairs sitting just outside them. The soldier tells Zack, "Please, take a seat. The council will see you shortly." Zack sits in the closest chair as the soldier goes through the pair of doors to tell the council of Zack's arrival. Zack waits impatiently, going over his speech again and again in his head the entire time until, about fifteen minutes later, the soldier comes back out and says, "Zack Branford, the council will see you now."

Zack stands up, says, "Thank you" to the soldier, and walks through the set of double doors. Inside is a large amphitheater containing a large table at the end, where the members of the council are sitting. There are ten members of the council, six men and four women, all older, at least in their fifties. Zack slowly walks in front of the table and faces the council.

One of the council members says, "Zack Branford, you are here because you have been found unfit for continuing the mission of hunting down the fugitive seraph, and according to Lieutenant

Miller, you believe that you should continue to work the mission. Is this correct?"

Zack answers, "Yes, sir."

"Even after the failed attempt to capture it at Aranea?"

"Yes, sir."

"On what grounds do you believe that we should let you continue this mission?"

"Because I'm still the one best suited for it. Because I have faced this thing twice now and survived when just about everyone else was killed. In their honor, I have to see this mission through to the end."

Another council member replies, "Well, it is true that you were the sole survivor of both facility attacks, except for Corporal Saren. And she came out of that mission a bit worse for wear, while you came out without a scratch. You do seem to have a knack for surviving against these things."

Another council member argued, "But he completely failed the mission. Obviously, he doesn't have what it takes to capture them. He may be able to survive against them, but we need to capture them."

One of the female council members rebukes, "Yes, but if nobody else can even survive against them, then they have no chance of capturing them. I say he stays on mission."

Zack replies, "Thank you, ma'am. I truly think that I alone can get this done. Please, you have to give me another chance."

Another council member says, "I think we need to ask ourselves if anyone else is able to do it. If nobody else can even survive against them, then we have no other choice but to use Mr. Branford here."

Another council member announces, "Well, if all arguments have been made, then I think we will bring this matter to a vote." She then turns to Zack and tells him, "A vote of at least six members is required for the motion to pass."

The council members then vote on the matter, verbally expressing their opinion with either a yes or no. The vote comes out eight to two in favor of letting Zack stay on mission. The final member to vote then announces, "This council has voted to let you stay on the mission. You will be given another chance to capture both fugitive seraph and bring them back to their rightful place. However, we cannot let you undergo this mission alone."

Zack thinks for a second then responds, "What about Corporal Saren? She has shown that she is capable, and she already has experience fighting these things, so she knows what to expect next time."

One of the female council members answers, "Yes, Corporal Saren has shown great potential in the field, and she has survived an encounter with one of the seraph. I believe that she would be an excellent choice."

Another council member interjects, "But she was seriously injured during said encounter. She barely got out alive. Perhaps someone with more experience in the field should accompany Mr. Branford?"

Another council member responds, "Yes, but now she will be better prepared to face the seraph because she knows what she's getting into. I say she should be the one to go with Mr. Branford."

Another council member says, "Let us bring the decision to a vote."

The council votes, and eight voted for having Amanda join Zack, with only two voting against it.

The previous council member announces, "It is decided. Mr. Branford, you will be allowed to continue the mission to hunt down and capture the escaped seraph, and Corporal Saren will accompany you. Is there any other business?"

Zack answers, "None, Your Honor."

The council member replies, "Then this meeting is adjourned."

The soldier that led Zack here leads him out of the council chamber and back to the hallway outside. Once there, he tells Zack, "Have a good day, sir," before leaving. Zack returns to his room and takes a nap.

About an hour later, someone knocks on Zack's door. Zack wakes up and opens the door to find another soldier waiting. The soldier says, "Mr. Branford, Lieutenant Miller would like to speak with you."

Zack exits his room and follows the soldier to Miller's office. Upon arrival, the soldier tells Zack, "Wait here," then walks inside. A few seconds later, he walks back out and says, "Lieutenant Miller will see you now." Zack then walks into the office and sits down on the chair in front of Miller's desk.

Miller says, "So I heard that you were allowed to remain on the assignment."

Zack replies, "I was, thank you for getting me an audience with the council."

"And I heard that Corporal Saren will be joining you."

"That is correct."

"Well, let me say congratulations."

"Thank you, it wouldn't have been possible without your help."

"When we get word on the whereabouts of the two escaped seraph, we will let you know."

"They're going to go after the final captive seraph, to set it free. We should be headed for that facility."

"The facility has already been informed of the situation, and measures have been taken to ensure the security of the captive seraph."

"That won't be enough. I need to be there."

"I know, which is why we're sending you there first thing tomorrow."

"What about Amanda?"

"She has made a full recovery from her injuries, and she will be joining you on your flight."

"Thank you. I promise I won't let you down this time."

"You better not, because the council will have my head if things go wrong again."

"That's not going to happen. You can be sure of that."

"I hope you're right. Now if you don't mind, I'm busy. I will send a soldier to your quarters tomorrow morning at 0600 to take you to the runway. Spend the rest of the day preparing. And good luck."

"Thanks, Miller, for everything," Zack says as he stands up. He then promptly walks out of the office and returns to his room.

He takes a nap until lunch, at which point he heads to the cafeteria. They are serving shredded chicken with peas and apple sauce. Zack waits several minutes in line, at which point he gets his lunch and sits in an empty area. He quickly eats his meal until Amanda walks in, gets her lunch, and sits down across from Zack.

Amanda greets Zack with "Hello, Zack."

"Oh, hi, Amanda," Zack replies.

"I'm so glad I got to see you. I can't thank you enough for saving my life back at Aranea."

"Don't mention it. I know you would've done the same."

"So I hear that we are going to be spending more time together."

"Yeah, the council agreed to give us another chance."

"I won't lie to you, I'm really nervous. I mean, those things are extremely dangerous! We could both be killed!"

"I know, but I refuse to leave the job undone. Besides, if we don't do it, then some other poor soul is going to have to, and even more people could be killed. I refuse to let that happen."

"Wow, you're so brave and noble."

"Please, I'm only doing what anyone else would do."

"But what of your family? Aren't you afraid of leaving them alone if you die?"

"Yes, but I know they would understand. What about your family?"

"Well, I don't like talking about it, but since you saved my life, I suppose you've earned the right to know. But I don't want to talk about it here. I'll stop by your room after lunch, okay?"

"Okay."

Zack finishes his lunch quickly and immediately heads to his room. He waits for a few minutes before Amanda arrives. When she does arrive, Zack sits down on his bed as Amanda tells her story.

Amanda begins, "I had a very happy family. We were all very close. But that changed when the war with Imperia broke out. It was about three years ago, when the Imperian military ransacked my home and killed my family. After that, I joined the military, looking to avenge my family."

Zack replies, "I'm so sorry. I had no idea."

"Thank you for your sympathy."

"You know, you didn't have to tell me if you didn't want to."

"It's all right. You saved my life. You earned the right to know. You know, I've never told anyone that story."

"Well, I'm glad you trusted me enough to tell me. It must have been hard to bring up such a painful memory."

"It's all right, really. I've had plenty of time to move on."

"Well, thanks for telling me."

"You're welcome. I'm…just going to go now. Bye."

"Goodbye," Zack says as Amanda leaves the room. He remains sitting on his bed, processing what Amanda had just told him. *She must really think you're something special*, he thinks to himself. He then lies on his bed and thinks about the coming days. *My second chance is almost here. I'd better not mess this up. I owe it to Miller to succeed this time.* He spends the next few hours thinking up plans to capture the seraph.

Eventually, dinner time came around, and Zack goes to the cafeteria to eat. They are serving Salisbury steak and mashed potatoes with gravy, along with a slice of yellow cake. Zack waits in line for a few minutes before getting his lunch and sitting in the nearest empty space. He quickly eats his meal and throws away his trash. Then he goes to the recreation room to watch television. Zack flips through dozens of channels, most of which have nothing good on, until he finally finds something he likes. It's an adult animated comedy show about a family that gets into a series of over-the-top adventures, called *Family in Excellus*. This episode is about the father getting accidentally sent back in time after stepping into his daughter's time machine (his daughter is a scientific genius), and his daughter is forced to go back in time to retrieve him. This is one of Zack's favorite episodes, one that he has seen half a dozen times already, but he still watches because he loves it. The episode is half an hour long, and Zack watches it in its entirety. Another episode is on after that, but now several other people have entered the room as well, and they want to watch something else.

Zack leaves the room and lets them watch whatever they want; he then goes to the gym to exercise. He spends several minutes running on a treadmill before going to the weighted bar to do some lifts. He puts one hundred pounds on the bar and is able to lift it with no trouble. He then adds another fifty pounds and is still able to lift it without any trouble. Finally, he adds a total of three hundred pounds to the bar, thus making it weigh almost four hundred pounds total, and he still lifts it with no trouble. He decides to not add any more weight to the bell, not wanting to risk injuring himself. He spends several minutes lifting the weights before Amanda walks in. She walks over to the dumbbells and picks up two weighing one hundred pounds each. Zack promptly leaves the gym, not wanting to disturb her.

He then decides to walk around the base, as he has not yet seen the base in its entirety. He steps outside and walks to every area of the base, except the ones that he's not allowed in, like the garage and the hangar. After walking for about an hour, Zack decides to head inside and return to his room. He takes off all his clothing and takes a shower before brushing his teeth and falling asleep.

CHAPTER 11

ZACK AWAKENS AT 0530 to the sound of his alarm. He quickly gets up, takes a shower, changes his clothes, and brushes his teeth. By the time he is done, it is 0556, almost time for the soldier to show up. He spends the next few minutes pacing back and forth across the room, thinking about his strategy for fighting the seraph. At 0600, a knock comes at Zack's door, and he opens it to see a soldier standing on the other side.

The soldier says, "Good morning, sir. I have come to escort you to the helipad."

Zack replies, "All right, lead on."

Zack closes his door behind him and follows the soldier to the helipad, where there is a helicopter waiting for him. He boards the helicopter, and right as he does, Amanda arrives. She boards the helicopter, and the two of them both strap on their harnesses as the helicopter starts up. After about a minute, the helicopter lifts off.

Zack asks Amanda, "Are you ready for this?"

Amanda answers, "About as ready as I can be. How about you?"

"Same here. I wonder how long it's going to take for the seraph to arrive."

"Hopefully not long. I want this mission to be over with as soon as possible."

"I know exactly how you feel. I also cannot wait to get this done and over with."

"I don't like being around those things. They give me the creeps."

"Yeah, me too. There's just something…off about them."

"You mean like the fact that they're trying to kill us?"

"No, not that. I've been around that plenty of times. I can't quite put my finger on it. They just feel…not right."

"I get it. The way they move is just so…unnatural, you know?"

"Yeah, I know. Regardless, I hope to put this whole business behind me as soon as possible."

"Yeah, me too."

Zack and Amanda spend the rest of the helicopter ride in silence, thinking and watching the landscape fly by.

After several hours, the helicopter finally reaches its destination, and slowly and delicately descends onto the helipad below. Zack and Amanda unbuckle their seat belts and carefully exit the helicopter. There is a soldier waiting for them on the helipad, and as soon as the helicopter lands, he instructs Zack and Amanda, "Follow me."

Zack and Amanda follow the soldier inside the base, which is a military research facility. The soldier leads Zack and Amanda to the main conference room, where a group of six officers is waiting for them.

One of the officers greets them, "Hello, and welcome to Heren, and welcome to our facility. I am General Max Armstrong, at your service. This is General Sam Worthington…"

General Worthington says, "Pleased to meet you."

General Armstrong continues, "This is Commander Ashton Brees…"

Commander Brees says, "Hello."

"This is Major Frederick Marlowe…"

Major Marlowe says, "A pleasure to make your acquaintance."

"This is Major John Kresnik…"

Major Kresnik says, "Hello, and welcome."

"And finally, this is Colonel Adrian Benson."

Colonel Benson says, "Pleased to meet you."

General Armstrong resumes, "And we all would like to offer you a warm welcome. Please, make yourselves comfortable. We know you won't be staying long, but we would like to make your stay as nice as possible. If there is anything you need, please, don't hesitate to ask. We would be happy to help you."

Amanda replies, "Thank you, but we just want to know what you guys have planned to catch the seraph."

General Worthington points to a map of the facility lying on the table in front of him and answers, "You are going to lure them into this hallway, and once they are there, we are going to throw knockout gas grenades at them. The men will all be equipped with Tasers as well, just in case."

Zack replies, "Tasers don't work on these things, neither do tranquilizers. Believe me, I've tried."

General Worthington asks, "Then what do you suppose we do?"

Zack replies, "Let me handle them. I've fought them before, and I understand how they fight. I believe that I can defeat them if given the chance."

Major Kresnik interjects, "Do you really expect us to just let you fight them alone? That's suicide, not to mention completely out of the question. The only way we can bring these things down is if we work together. Our men are trained to handle any situation, and they will get the job done."

Zack says, "With all due respect, Major, I doubt that your men have been trained to handle this. Nothing can truly prepare you for going up against one of those things, much less two. We thought our soldiers were ready to fight them as well, and now they are all dead. I am the only one who has fought them and survived unharmed. I am the only one that can stop them. You have to let me try."

"We cannot allow you to go up against those things alone. We can only defeat them if we fight together. I can assure you, our men are prepared for any threat, and they will get the job done."

"All right, fine, we'll do it your way."

"Good, now, if that's out of the way, can we get back to discussing strategy here?"

"All right."

"Commander Brees, if you would."

Commander Brees steps forward and announces, "This will be our strategy for the upcoming mission." He points to the entrance on the map and continues, "Mr. Branford and Corporal Saren, you will lure both of the seraph to this entrance and lead them into the facility. Once they are inside, you will lead them to this hallway here." He points to a hallway on the map, then continues, "We will have a dozen soldiers waiting there, and once you have lured the seraph there, you will get out of harm's way so that we can use knockout gas grenades. The soldiers will also be equipped with Tasers and tranquilizer darts, just in case. With all their combined strength, they will be able to safely subdue the seraph. Then they will be put in stasis pods to ensure that they do not wake up. After that is taken care of, plans will be set up for the transportation of the seraph back to their rightful places. The rest of the soldiers have already been briefed on this mission. Do either of you have any questions?"

Amanda asks, "Yeah, are you sure that trying to subdue both of the seraph at once in the same place is safe? Wouldn't it be better to lure each seraph to a different location and subdue them each individually?"

Colonel Benson steps forward and answers, "We have sufficient manpower and weaponry that we can take them both down at once. Don't worry, everything will go smoothly."

Zack asks, "They will be going after the seraph located in this facility. Do you have it stored in a safe location so that they can't get to it?"

"Yes, we have it stored within this vault,"—Benson points to a vault within the secure storage area of the facility—"which is made of the strongest metal on the planet. There is no way the seraph will be able to get access to it."

"Okay, that should be enough to stop them. I don't have any other questions. What about you, Amanda?"

Amanda answers, "No, I don't have any more questions either. This sounds like a solid plan."

General Worthington says, "Well, if there are no more questions, then this meeting is adjourned. We will let you two know when the seraph have been spotted. Until then, make yourselves comfortable."

Amanda replies, "Thank you very much. It was nice meeting all of you, and I hope you all have a good day."

"You two have a good day as well."

Zack and Amanda leave the room and see two soldiers waiting for them. The first says, "Hello, Mr. Branford. Please follow me," and leads Zack to his quarters while the other says, "Hello, Corporal Saren. Please follow me," and leads Amanda to her quarters. Zack follows the soldier until he reaches his quarters.

He looks around for about a minute then asks the soldier, "Could you show me where the cafeteria is, please?"

The soldier answers, "You mean the break room? We don't actually have a cafeteria here. Everyone brings their own meals."

"Yes, the break room, then."

"Of course, sir. Follow me." The soldier leads Zack to the break room.

Zack looks around for a few seconds before turning back to the soldier and saying, "Thank you for your help."

The soldier asks, "Is there anything else you need?"

"Yes, could you show me the route that I am going to be taking on this mission?"

"Certainly, sir. Right this way." The soldier then leads Zack to the entrance of the facility and says, "This is where you will start the mission. Once the seraph arrive, you will go down this hallway." The soldier points behind him as he says this. "You will then take the following route." He leads Zack down a series of hallways until they reach the point where the soldiers will be stationed, at which point the soldier says, "And this is where you will lead the seraph. The soldiers will be stationed here. Is there anything else you need?"

"No, thank you."

"You have a good day, sir."

"Thank you, you too."

The soldier leaves, and Zack goes back to his room, where he takes a nap for several hours. There is a knock on his door, which wakes him up, and when he answers it, there is a soldier on the other side who says, "It's time for lunch."

Zack walks down to the break room, where several dozen personnel are sitting, eating, and talking. When he gets there, the soldier tells Zack, "Please, sit down, sir. Someone will be along to serve you shortly." Zack sits down at the nearest empty space and waits for a few minutes before another soldier walks up to him and says, "Good afternoon, sir. I will be serving you today. To start you off, would a glass of milk be okay?"

Zack answers, "Yes, that would be fine."

"Okay. Now we do not have our own cafeteria here, so I apologize for the lack of options. We just got some food flown in here especially for you and Corporal Saren. Would you like some spaghetti and garlic bread?"

"Yes, that sounds lovely."

"Okay. And finally, would you like a piece of pumpkin pie?"

"Yes."

"I shall have your meal shortly." The soldier leaves, and Zack waits for a couple of minutes, during which Amanda arrives and sits across from Zack.

As Amanda sits down, she says, "Hello, Zack."

Zack replies, "Hello, Amanda. How are you doing?"

"I'm fine. How about you?"

"I'm doing well. How are you liking the facility?"

"It's okay, nothing too special as far as facilities like this go. Well, apart from containing a seraph, of course. What about you? How do you like this place?"

"It's pretty nice. It's a lot like the places I visited in Excellus."

"You've visited other places like this?"

"Yeah, I became a safety inspector for government facilities like this after a quit the military."

"Oh. How was that?"

"It was good. Not too difficult, good pay. Just the kind of job I needed. What about you? What are you going to do once you get out of the military?"

"I'm not leaving the military until I retire. I rather enjoy it."

"Oh. Well…good for you then. I'm glad that you found something that makes you happy."

"Thanks. So how did you like it in the military?"

"I liked it pretty well."

"Then why did you quit?"

"Didn't you hear Miller say it when you first met me? It was because of the incident at Marsden that I'd rather not discuss."

"Okay. I'm sorry I brought it up."

"It's okay, just please don't do it again."

Zack began to remember the incident, despite wanting to bury it forever. Soon after the war against Imperia, Zack was sent on a mission to the town of Marsden to deal with a group of terrorists who had taken the townspeople hostage. Zack's mission was to scout out the locations of the terrorists and the hostages. However, he wasn't told that there were drones in the air. After Zack gave the locations to headquarters, the drones bombed them, killing all the terrorists and the hostages. The government covered it up by saying that the terrorists suicide bombed the city. Thus, Zack became disillusioned with the military and promptly left, pursuing a more peaceful career.

A soldier walked up to Amanda to take her order, then promptly left, saying, "Your food will be here shortly," as he went.

Amanda then asks, "So what are you going to do when this mission is over?"

Zack answers, "Go back to my job. Go back to my life. Just go back to what I was doing before. What about you?"

"Same."

The soldier who took Zack's order returns with Zack's food, along with plastic utensils. Zack starts eating his meal, and Amanda receives hers as Zack is eating his. They both eat their meals in silence, then they throw their utensils away. Zack and Amanda then both say bye to each other and return to their rooms.

Zack lies in his bed and goes to sleep.

CHAPTER 12

AT 0725, ZACK is awoken by the sound of a knock on his door. He answers it and finds a soldier waiting for him.

The soldier says, "Mr. Branford, you're wanted in the conference room."

Zack responds, "Okay, give me a minute." He quickly changes his clothes and brushes his teeth before walking out the door and following the soldier to the conference room.

Once they arrive, Zack is greeted by General Worthington, who says, "Hello, Zack," as he walks in. The other five officers are there as well, as is Amanda and about a dozen soldiers. The officers are all wearing headsets. General Worthington continues, "Everyone, the time has come. Satellites have spotted the seraph just a couple miles away. They will be here in an hour at most. We have to stop them here, or who knows how much more damage they could do. Zack, Amanda, do you want me to go over the plan one more time, just to be safe?"

Zack answers, "Yes, please."

"Zack, Amanda, you will be stationed outside, and you will lead the seraph to this entrance." General Worthington points to the main entrance on the map on the table and continues, "Once inside, you will lead them to this hallway"—he points to a hallway on the map—"where we will have a dozen men ready in waiting. Once the seraph are there, you two will quickly move out of the way while our soldiers toss knockout gas grenades at the seraph. The men will also be equipped with Tasers, as will you two, just in case that becomes necessary. With our combined might, we will quickly subdue the seraph and store them in cryogenic chambers to ensure that they do not reawaken. Are there any questions from you two?"

Zack asks, "Have you evacuated all non-essential personnel from the base? I don't want any of them to be put in harm's way."

"Don't worry. All personnel not involved in the mission have left the building. It's just us here."

"Good. I don't want there to be any unnecessary casualties."

Amanda asks, "Can we be shown where exactly we will be leading the seraph? I want to know where we're going beforehand."

General Worthington answers, "That is a great idea. Corporal Jennings?"

One of the soldiers steps forward and says, "Yes, sir?"

"Show these two the route that they will be taking to lure the seraph to you. Just be quick about it, and answer any questions they may have."

"Sir, yes, sir!" the soldier exclaims before turning to Zack and Amanda and instructing them, "Follow me!"

Corporal Jennings leads them out of the room and down a set of hallways until eventually reaching the main entrance of the facility. He then tells them, "This is where you will start."

Amanda asks, "Is there any particular spot that you want us to be?"

The soldier answers, "Yes, right here at the entrance. We want to make sure that the seraph see you here and enter through this doorway."

"Okay, thanks. Please continue."

"Follow me." Corporal Jennings leads them back inside and through another series of hallways and corridors. Zack and Amanda study their surroundings the entire time, paying attention to every sign, trying to memorize every detail so that they won't get lost during the chase. Eventually, they reach the spot where the soldiers are going to be stationed, and Corporal Jennings tells them, "This is where we will be waiting. Just lead the seraph here and let us do the rest. Are there any questions?"

Zack asks, "Where do you want us to go once the seraph have reached this spot?"

Corporal Jennings answers, "Just go somewhere that's out of the way. Maybe just run a bit down the hall that way." Corporal Jennings points down the hallway. "Just as long as you're not in our way. Are there any other questions?"

Amanda asks, "Will we be given gas masks, just in case, since you guys are going to be using knockout gas?"

Jennings answers, "I believe so. You will have to ask the officers to be sure, but I'm pretty sure that you will. The men and I will definitely be equipped with gas masks, since we will be close to the gas when it is deployed. Now are there any more questions?"

Zack and Amanda are silent, indicating that they have no more questions. Corporal Jennings then announces, "If there are no more questions, then we must return to the conference room." He leads Zack and Amanda back to the conference room, where the officers are looking at a screen on the wall, showing the movement of the seraph as they head toward the base.

As the group arrives, Jennings says, "Sirs, we are back."

The officers turn away from the screen and look at Zack, Amanda, and Jennings, then General Worthington says, "Thank you, Jennings. You may go gear up now."

Jennings exclaims, "Thank you, sir," then leaves.

Amanda asks, "Sir, what are we going to be equipped with for this mission?"

Worthington answers, "You two are going to be equipped with swords made out of the strongest metal on the planet, along with Tasers, body armor, and gas masks. We want to ensure your safety as much as possible on this mission. Do either of you have any other questions?"

Zack asks, "If possible, could we get another tour of the route we will be taking before the mission starts?"

"If there is time, then yes. It's a good idea, we want to make sure you two don't get lost during the mission. That would be catastrophic. Any other questions before you two get geared up?"

Zack answers, "I don't have any."

Amanda responds, "Neither do I."

General Worthington replies, "Let's get you two geared up. I'll show you to your gear." He leads them down a series of hallways until they come upon a small room in the corner of the facility. He says, "Your gear is in this room. Wait here just a minute." He goes into the room. Zack and Amanda wait for a few seconds before General Worthington steps back out and says, "There's someone else in there. We'll have to wait for them to finish." Zack and Amanda wait about a minute until Corporal Jennings steps out, decked out in full military gear.

Corporal Jennings says, "I'm done," as he steps out.

General Worthington then tells Zack and Amanda, "Now it's your turn. One of you step inside and get geared up."

Amanda says, "I'll go," before walking into the room. Zack waits for a couple of minutes for Amanda to finish. As she walks out of the room, fully geared, she says, "Zack, your turn."

Zack steps into the room. It is small and rectangular shaped, with white walls made out of concrete blocks. The gear is sitting in the corner of the room. Zack walks over to it and starts gearing up. First, he puts on the vest, which sits surprisingly comfortably on his torso, then he picks up the sword, which is held in a large sheath made out of alund. He mounts the sheath strap over his shoulder, putting the sword on his back. He then picks up the Taser and puts it in his pocket. Finally, he takes the gas mask and puts it on top of his head, so that it wouldn't obscure his vision.

After he has finished gearing up, Zack steps out of the room. As he walks out, he tells General Worthington, "I'm ready."

General Worthington replies, "Everyone is ready. The soldiers are all at their stations and waiting to receive their orders. Oh, I almost forgot." He pulls out two small headsets and gives one to Zack and one to Amanda. As he does this, he says, "I'm supposed to give you these so that you can communicate with each other and with the units."

Zack and Amanda each take a headset and place them on their heads. Zack has to take his gas mask off first before putting his on.

General Worthington continues, "Now that that's out of the way, if you would both kindly follow me, please. We need to get back to the conference room to check on the progress of the seraph." He leads them both back to the conference room, where the other five officers are intently looking at the screen on the wall. He looks at the screen as well, which shows a video of the two seraph running through a field close to the facility, and next to this is a countdown showing how close they are to the facility, as well as an approximate length of time before they reach it. Currently, it says they are ten miles away, with an estimated time of arrival of ten minutes.

Zack asks, "Can we get a quick tour of the route we will be taking before the seraph arrive?"

General Worthington answers, "Yes. Follow me." He quickly leads them to the entrance of the facility and says, "You two will be stationed here. When the seraph arrive, you will lead them down this hallway,"—he points down the hallway behind them and continues—"where you will lead them down the path we are about to take. Now, pay attention you two, as I am going to have to do this quickly. Follow me." He leads them down the path they will be taking to reach the soldiers. Once again, Zack and Amanda pay extremely close attention to the signs and other distinguishing features of the path, taking care to memorize every detail to ensure that they do not get lost. Eventually, they reach the soldiers, and General Worthington says, "And this is where the soldiers are stationed, and where you two will lead the seraph. Do either of you have any last-minute questions?"

Zack and Amanda both shake their heads, indicating that they have no further questions.

General Worthington continues, "Get back to the entrance, quick. They'll be here any minute. I'm going back to the conference room with the rest of the officers. We'll let you know when they arrive." He goes back to the conference room.

Zack and Amanda return to the entrance to the facility. They wait patiently to receive word from the officers of the seraphs' arrival.

Zack's mind is racing with thoughts of the seraph and of the mission. *This is my last chance,* he thinks to himself. *I have to stop them here. Miller went to a lot of work to get you here. You'd better not screw this up.* He begins remembering his previous battles with the seraph. *The way they move is insane. There's no way any person could hope to match their speed. Yet somehow, I can. I don't know how, but I can. It's like there's something inside me that compels my body to move with unnatural speed. I have no idea what it is, but it sure has been helpful.*

Zack begins noticing the slight breeze of the wind. It feels cool, calming, and gentle on his skin. It helps him to relax, and suddenly, he notices that his breathing and heart rate have slowed slightly. That will soon change, as when the seraph show up, he will be fighting for his life.

As Zack is thinking about all this, a call comes from the headset. "This is General Worthington. The seraph are about to reach the facility. All units, be on full alert. This is the moment we have been waiting for. Do your country proud."

Zack begins to tense up, and his breathing and heart rate increase. He waits, patiently, for what seems like an eternity, for the inevitable confrontation. He looks over at Amanda, who looks very calm and collected, but who, undoubtedly, is just as nervous as he is. For a few moments, all is calm and quiet.

Suddenly, Zack gets another splitting headache. He puts his hand on his forehead and lets out a small, quiet grunt of pain. He can feel his heartbeat in his head; it feels like his head is about to be split open.

Then suddenly, the seraph appear. They rush the entrance, Zack and Amanda quickly fall back into the base. The seraph follow them closely as they run down the series of corridors and hallways to get to the place where the soldiers are stationed. They are careful to follow all the directions given to them, remembering every twist and turn along the way.

Finally, they reach the soldiers. They then quickly leap out of the way just as the soldiers throw their canisters of knockout gas at the seraph. Zack and Amanda quickly put on their gas masks.

Then there is stillness. For a few seconds, there is nothing except the hissing of the canisters releasing their gas. Everyone waits patiently, tensely, to see if the gas worked and knocked out the seraph.

Suddenly, the seraph leap out of the gas and begin cutting down the soldiers, one by one. The soldiers try to fight back, several managing to fire off the Tasers, but to no avail. They all miss or are quickly shrugged off, and the seraph resume their killing spree until every last soldier is dead. Zack and Amanda look on in horror as the soldiers are all sliced into bloody pieces.

However, they soon spring into action, drawing their swords and running straight at the seraph. The golden-haired seraph parries their attacks and tells the other seraph, "Go, I'll hold them off." The male seraph nods and runs off. Zack tries to follow him, but the female seraph blocks his path. Zack, Amanda, and the seraph have a furious battle, trading blows and blocking each of them, with Zack constantly having to step in front of Amanda to shield her from the seraph's blows due to her immense speed. During the battle, the seraph manages to knock the gas mask off of Zack's face, and he begins breathing in the knockout gas. However, for some reason, it doesn't cause Zack to fall unconscious. Zack doesn't understand how, but he doesn't have time to think about it, as the seraph takes the opportunity to punch Amanda in the cheek, knocking her to the ground. Zack quickly leaps between them to protect Amanda, preventing the seraph from finishing her off. Zack pushes the seraph away and rushes forward with a quick thrust, but the seraph manages to step out of the way, and counters with a hard punch straight to Zack's gut. Zack is left reeling, and the seraph goes in for the finishing blow, but Zack manages to block it just in time. With his stomach in pain and his head still throbbing, Zack tries a desperate swipe with his sword, but to no avail, as the seraph easily blocks the attack. Meanwhile, Amanda manages to make her way to her feet and unleashes a flurry of slashes, but the seraph easily blocks all these attacks before punching her in the stomach, grabbing her by the neck, and throwing her across the hallway. By this point, the knockout gas has dissipated, so Zack can now see clearly to fight. However, this doesn't stop the seraph from being able to anticipate and block every attack that he throws at her. Amanda stands back up and runs to Zack's side, the two of them breathing heavily and reeling in pain, staring the seraph down. The seraph rushes forward, unleashing a barrage of attacks at Zack, who somehow manages to block them all. The seraph then punches Zack in the right cheek, knocking him to the floor. Then turning her attention to Amanda, the seraph slowly walks toward her, methodical and with great purpose. She raises her sword, ready to deliver the finishing blow and kill Amanda, but before she can, Zack gets back to his feet and thrusts his sword straight through the seraph's chest. The seraph's eyes widen in shock and horror before she falls to her knees. She stays there for a few seconds, breathing heavily, with the sword still sticking inside her body, before she collapses to the ground. Zack yanks the sword out of her body, and he and Amanda stare at the corpse for a few seconds, blood oozing out of the seraph's wound and onto the ground.

Zack and Amanda both breathe a sigh of relief while still breathing heavily from the battle. Then an alarm goes off, and Zack and Amanda look at each other with horrified expressions on their faces, as they both know that the alarm can mean only one thing.

They rush to the vault where the final seraph is being held as fast as they possibly can, but when they get there, they realize they are too late, as they find the vault door sliced open and the final captive seraph missing. They then rush to the conference room, where they find the officers all alive and well, waiting for Zack and Amanda to return and bring news of the mission.

Zack says to General Worthington, "Sir, we managed to kill one of the seraph, but the other got away, and released the final seraph. All of the soldiers are dead."

General Worthington replies, "What? How?"

"That's not important right now. What's important is that we catch the seraph still out there. We need your help."

"What can we do?"

"Find the location of the two seraph and get us a helicopter and a plot to go after them."

"Okay. You got it." General Worthington runs out of the room.

Zack and Amanda wait for several minutes before General Worthington returns.

As soon as he gets back, General Worthington tells Zack and Amanda, "I've made some calls. There is a helicopter pilot on the way, and we have spotted the seraph on satellite. Wherever they go, we'll know."

Zack responds, "Thank you."

"Okay, so it's going to take about an hour for the pilot to get here. Tell me what happened to my men."

Zack explains what happened during the mission.

General Worthington bows his head and says, "Dear god. That's horrible. Nobody should have to die like that, especially men as good as them."

The rest of the officers bow their heads as well, as a sign of respect for the fallen.

Zack and Amanda then wait for the helicopter pilot to arrive. While they wait, Zack thinks about the battle that he just endured.

He thinks to himself, *Well, it looks like they can be killed just like a human. At least now we know. This information will come in very handy later.*

Zack spends the rest of the hour thinking to himself until, finally, the pilot arrives.

CHAPTER 13

WHEN THE PILOT arrives, she asks General Worthington, "I got your call. What's this about?"

The pilot is a young woman, probably in her mid-twenties, with long blond hair. She is wearing a black t-shirt with a picture from a movie and jeans.

General Worthington says, "We need your help for a top-secret mission. I called you because you are the best pilot we have available." He points at Zack and Amanda and continues, "I need you to fly these two to find two fugitives that are on the run. Can you do that for me?"

The pilot raises one eyebrow and asks, "Finding fugitives? Isn't that more of a job for the police?"

"These fugitives are...special. That's all you need to know. Can you please help us out here?"

"All right, just give me a minute to suit up."

"Thank you. Go get ready, and please be quick."

"Can do, sir."

The pilot leaves to put her flight suit on.

General Worthington tells Zack and Amanda, "That's Jessica Silverman. She's one of our best pilots."

Zack replies, "Good to know."

A few minutes later, Jessica returns, now wearing a brownish flight suit and a large pilot's helmet, and she says, "I'm ready. Are you guys ready?"

Zack and Amanda both nod.

Jessica then says, "Let's go."

Jessica leads Zack and Amanda to the helipad outside the facility. There, they board a small, black helicopter. Jessica enters first and starts up the engines as Zack and Amanda enter and put on their harnesses. After a couple of minutes, the helicopter roars to life and lifts off the ground.

Zack and Amanda put on their helmets, which have headsets built into them, and Jessica says, "All right, command is giving me the coordinates of the targets as I speak. It will take us about an hour to reach them. Until then, just sit back, relax, and enjoy the ride. We have nice weather today, so it'll be smooth flying."

Zack responds, "Thank you. Just get us there as quickly as possible. We need to get this done fast."

"I'll do what I can."

The helicopter speeds off in the direction of the seraph. As they are flying, Zack and Amanda can hear command constantly updating Jessica on the coordinates of the seraph and can feel Jessica making slight adjustments to their flight paths in accordance with the new coordinates.

After about an hour of flying, they finally reach the seraph. As soon as they come into view, Jessica says, "I have a visual on the fugitives. I'm moving to intercept."

Command responds with, "Roger, move to intercept."

Zack starts to get a headache again, causing him to wince in pain.

Amanda notices and asks Zack, "Are you okay, Zack?"

Zack answers, "Yeah, I'm fine."

"Are you sure? You don't look so well."

"I said I'm fine!" Zack exclaims. Amanda is taken aback, and Zack says, "I'm sorry. But I'm fine, really."

"All right, if you say so."

Jessica flies the helicopter directly over the seraph and quickly lowers it to the ground. Zack and Amanda quickly remove their helmets and harnesses and jump out of the helicopter.

The female seraph turns around to face Zack and Amanda, while the male seraph continues running. Zack and Amanda both unsheathe their swords and prepare for battle. The seraph rushes forward and swings ferociously, but Zack is able to deftly block the attack. They hold that pose for a few seconds before pushing each other away. Zack counterattacks with a wide swing, but the seraph manages to duck under it and punch Zack in the stomach. Zack winces in pain, and the seraph takes the opportunity to swipe at Zack. Amanda pushes Zack out of the way while narrowly avoiding the attack herself. The seraph quickly uppercuts Amanda straight in the chin, knocking her back several feet and to the ground. Zack recovers from the punch and attacks the seraph with a quick thrust, which she quickly sidesteps to avoid. She then follows up with an upward swipe, which Zack blocks. Zack tries to punch her in the cheek, but she catches his hand, twists his arm, and then quickly lowers her other arm down onto his elbow, breaking his arm. Zack lets out a sharp scream of pain, and the seraph takes the opportunity to hit Zack in the back of the head with the hilt of her sword. Zack collapses to the ground, and the seraph stabs him in the stomach. Zack lets out a grunt of pain and starts coughing up blood.

Amanda quickly gets back to her feet and, seizing the opportunity, plunges her sword straight into the seraph's chest and quickly pulls it back out. The seraph lets out a sharp cry before collapsing to the ground, blood pouring from the wound.

Amanda then turns her attention to Zack, turning his body so that he is laying on his side. She frantically says, "It's okay. You're okay. You're going to be okay."

Zack looks at Amanda, who is frantically trying to stop the bleeding by pressing her hands firmly on the wound but being careful not to remove the sword to slow the bleeding. Zack lets out a low sigh as he slowly slips into unconsciousness.

CHAPTER 14

ZACK SLOWLY AWAKENS in a hospital bed, hooked up to medical equipment and surrounded by doctors. He hears the heartbeat monitor beeping next to him as he looks around the room. He tries to lift his arms but finds that they are securely fastened to the bed, then he finds out that his legs are as well.

Zack calls out, "What's going on? Why am I strapped to the bed? Somebody please tell me what's going on!"

Several of the doctors turn to face Zack, and one of them says, "He's awake. Put him back under—now."

The mask on Zack's face begins to fill with anesthesia, and he slowly drifts back into unconsciousness.

When he wakes back up, he is still strapped down to the hospital bed, but this time, he is in a different room, with only two doctors this time. He sees x-ray pictures posted on the wall next to him, and he notices that he is still in extreme pain from the battle.

Zack once again calls out to the doctors, "Hey! What's going on here?"

The doctors turn to face Zack, and one of them says, "He's awake again. Call Dr. Strauss."

The other doctor leaves, and the remaining doctor slowly walks toward Zack. He says, "Calm down. You were injured during the battle. We are getting the doctor now."

The doctor is old, looking to be in his seventies, with a bald head and wrinkles covering his face. On his coat hangs a keycard that says, "Samuel Harvey, MD."

Zack asks, "Why am I strapped down to the bed?"

The doctor ignores Zack's question and walks to the other end of the room to grab his notes.

Zack asks again, "Hey, why am I strapped down to the table?"

The doctor continues ignoring Zack and looking at his notes. Zack gives up on trying to get an answer and lays his head down on the pillow.

After several minutes, another doctor enters the room. He is in his forties, with short blonde hair, wearing jeans and a lab coat. On his coat, a keycard saying "Eli Strauss, MD" is hung from the pocket on his breast area. Dr. Strauss talks to Dr. Harvey, but Zack cannot hear what they are saying. After about a minute, Dr. Strauss stops talking to Dr. Harvey and turns his attention to Zack.

Dr. Strauss says, "Mr. Branford, you suffered severe injuries during your battle. Please rest and wait for your wounds to heal."

Zack asks, "Why am I strapped down to this bed?"

"Because we cannot trust you to not attack us."

"Attack you? Why would I attack you?"

"Well, after what happened at Mt. Hormel, we can no longer trust you."

"Mt. Hormel? What does that have to do with this?"

"We found the security footage of the attack. We know what you did."

"Yeah, I tried to stop the seraph."

"After you freed it and killed many of our soldiers in the process."

"What? What are you talking about? I didn't free the seraph."

"Yes, you did. We have security camera footage that shows you doing it. We just found it a few days ago, and we have kept you strapped down ever since."

"A few days ago? How long have I been here?"

"About a week. Your wounds were pretty severe when you got here, but we have managed to heal them up rather nicely."

"Take these straps off of me."

"I'm sorry, I cannot do that. You are far too dangerous to let roam. We need to keep you secure for everyone's safety."

"I'm not a danger to any of you. I would never hurt you."

"I'm sorry, that's a risk we just cannot take."

Zack gives up trying to convince the doctor to release his shackles. He instead focuses his attention on the x-ray images, particularly the one of his head. There was something off about it, but Zack couldn't put his finger on it. After staring intently at the image for several minutes, he eventually gives up trying to discern what was wrong with it, as he couldn't figure it out.

Suddenly, a short, black-haired woman comes bursting into the room, shouting, "We're under attack!"

Doctor Strauss asks her, "Who's attacking us?"

The woman replies, "I don't know! Some…strange man with a sword. He's killing everyone!"

Zack asks, "This man with the sword, does he have long, brown hair?"

The woman replies, "Yeah, how did you know?"

"Doctor Strauss, you have to let me go—now!"

Doctor Strauss asks, "Why?"

Zack answers, "Because I know what we're dealing with, and only I can stop it!"

"I can't let you go. You might start attacking us too."

"I'm telling you, I won't attack you. Now please take these shackles off me."

Suddenly, Zack starts to hear screaming from outside the room. Zack thinks to himself, *The seraph, it has found me. But how? And why has it come here just for me?* Zack struggles to try to break his bonds, but to no avail. Suddenly, he starts getting a headache again, the worst one yet. Zack lets out a scream of pain, for the headache is overwhelmingly painful, like someone is drilling directly into his brain.

Doctor Harvey leaves the room to try to see what's going on. A few seconds later, he is violently thrown back into the room.

The seraph slowly walks into the room and then proceeds to quickly dispatch of the two doctors, slicing through them like a hot knife through butter. It then turns its attention toward Zack, slowly walking toward him.

Zack continues to struggle, but he still cannot release his shackles. Zack then notices that his headache is gone.

Zack hears in his mind, *I knew there was something…different about you. I knew that you weren't like the humans, I just didn't know how. But now I do.*

Zack looks at the seraph and says, "Are you…talking to me? In my mind? How?"

Zack hears the same voice in his mind, *Yes, I am talking to you. As for how, well, think about it. All seraph share a telepathic link to each other. I am able to communicate with you in your mind. So…*

Zack's eyes open wide, and a shocked expression comes over his face. He then says, "No…"

That's right. You are also a seraph.

"But how is that possible? I thought all of the seraph were captured."

So did I, but it seems that one managed to escape. Your mother.

"My mother? My mother is a human who lives a normal life. She can't possibly be a seraph."

Those people you grew up with are not your real parents. They merely found you after your mother left you.

"No, that can't be true. They would have told me if they weren't my real parents. I know they would have told me."

But they didn't. You've spent your whole life, never knowing the truth about what you really are.

"Yeah, well how do you know so much about me?"

I spoke with your mother just a few days ago. She told me everything.

"Why would she tell you anything?"

Because us seraph have to stick together, which is the reason why I am here. I want you to join me.

"Join you in what?"

Living our own lives, away from the humans.

"Why would I abandon those that I have known for my whole life? Why would I give up everything I have?"

Because I can see inside you. Inside your head. I can see your true thoughts, and I can see that you are not truly happy with your life. Come with me, and I can fix that. You can have the life you truly want.

"I'm sorry, but I'm going to have to decline. You've killed many innocent people, and I don't want anything to do with you."

I would hardly call any of them innocent. Do you see what they have done to us? They used us as playthings for years. They are all sick and twisted. But not us. We are better than them.

"Not all of them are bad. There are many good humans, who care for and help others."

That may be true, but they would still never accept us. They are full of fear, and that fear makes them do terrible things.

"They could learn to be better. They could learn to accept us."

No, they won't ever see us as anything but a threat to them. They will always fear and hate us. We have no place among them, which is why we must live without them, apart from them.

"You do what you wish, but I am still going to live with them."

That is a very foolish decision. Now that they know what you are, they will not accept you either.

"I don't care what you think. You killed so many people. You're a monster."

I only killed those people because I had to, to escape captivity and to help my brothers and sisters do the same. But these humans, they kill all the time out of greed and selfishness. They are unworthy of life.

"Yes, humans can be terrible sometimes, but they are also often kind and merciful and caring."

Enough of this. This argument is going nowhere. Come and live with me, and you can finally be happy.

"I'm sorry, but no. I'm staying with the humans, and that's final."

Then you leave me no choice.

The seraph raises its blade, ready to kill Zack. However, Zack manages to break free of his shackles and roll off of the bed as the seraph swings his sword down, slicing the bed in half. Zack immediately stands up and faces the seraph. He then quickly punches the seraph in the gut, staggering it for a few seconds, giving him just enough time to run into the hallway next to his room.

Zack looks around for a few seconds, unsure of where to go, when the seraph suddenly comes bursting out of the room. He takes several swipes at Zack, but he is able to dodge them all and kick him in the groin, knocking him down to his knees. Zack then runs from the seraph as quickly as he can, closely looking at signs along the way to figure out which way to go to get out of the hospital. He runs down several hallways before finding the staircase leading down.

Suddenly, the seraph shows up again, barreling down the hallway after Zack. Zack turns around the corner and ducks into a nearby room, looking to hide from the seraph. It is a patient's room, with a patient inside, sleeping. Zack starts getting a headache again as the seraph slowly walks down the hallway, scanning all of the rooms it passes by, but it doesn't see Zack. It walks right by the room that he is in, not going inside. Zack waits several minutes to make sure that the seraph has passed, and quietly exits the room, turns the corner again, and goes down the staircase.

Now on the first floor of the hospital, Zack looks for the way to the exit. He begins scanning the nearby signs, but none of them say which way the entrance or exit is. He decides to run straight down the hallway and hope he finds something at the other end. No such luck, as it just leads to a four-way intersection of two hallways. Zack takes a right, but stops once he hears the seraph's footsteps nearby. He once again ducks into a nearby room, this time a janitor's closet, and waits several minutes for the sound to pass.

Meanwhile, the seraph is patrolling the first floor, slowly walking down the hallways to try to find Zack, but with no luck. He tries to find Zack with telepathy, but for some reason, he cannot understand, he is unable to. He periodically stops to listen for the sound of footsteps but is unable to hear any. So he continues his search for Zack, wanting to kill him for refusing his offer.

Zack listens intently for the sound of footsteps but is unable to hear them anymore, so he quietly exits the janitor's closet and continues down the hallway, making sure to look at all of the signs to see if any of them point toward the entrance or exit. After running through several hallways, he finally sees a sign pointing to the entrance of the hospital. Zack passes dozens of corpses along the way, victims of the seraph's massacre. He runs down several more hallways, stopping periodically to listen for the sound of the seraph's footsteps but not hearing anything.

He eventually makes his way to the hospital entrance, where the military is ready and waiting. Zack hides as a number of soldiers run past him.

Suddenly, the seraph comes into view, and the soldiers immediately open fire upon it; however, it is able to dodge all of their gunfire and slice them apart. The seraph then continues to the entrance, where dozens more soldiers are waiting for it. The seraph slices through these soldiers as well before running off.

Zack uses the confusion as an opportunity to sneak out of the hospital without any soldiers or the seraph noticing him. He runs down the street and in front of a car driving toward him. The car is dark red and looks several years old. The driver stops suddenly, narrowly avoiding hitting Zack. Zack walks around to the driver's side door, opens it, throws the driver out, gets in the car, and drives off.

CHAPTER 15

Zack drives for hours until he finally reaches his destination, his home. There, he hopes to meet his parents and ask them if they are his real parents.

Zack sees his home in the distance but also sees that it is surrounded by soldiers.

They must have suspected that I would come here, Zack thought to himself. *I mean, it does make sense that this would be the first place that I would go. That means that they know that I escaped the hospital. This could be tricky.*

Zack stops the car away from the house and watches it intently. He counts about thirty soldiers, not including any that might be inside the house. He also watches their patrol patterns, looking for any openings that might get him inside without having to fight anyone. Thinking that he has found one, he sprints toward the house before ducking behind the animal pen, where his parents keep all of their farm animals. He waits for several minutes for a couple of soldiers to pass by before quietly sneaking his way through. He then hides behind a large tree in the backyard, waiting for another soldier to pass by, then sneaks past him. Then he hides behind a natural gas tank and waits for two more soldiers to cross each other's paths and continue walking. Once they are past, he sneaks by them and finally manages to reach his house. He peeks through a nearby window and sees two soldiers in the living room and one in the kitchen. He then quietly goes around the house to the garage and peeks through the window on the door there. There is one soldier in the garage.

Looks like I won't get through without confrontation, Zack thinks to himself as he formulates a plan for quietly taking out the guard.

After thinking through his strategy, Zack quietly opens the door and enters the garage. Thankfully, the guard is facing away from Zack, so he is able to sneak in without the soldier noticing. He quietly sneaks up behind the guard and wraps his arm around the soldier's neck, while also putting his hand over the soldier's mouth to muffle his cries for help until the soldier is rendered unconscious. Zack then moves the soldier out of the way so nobody will find him before opening the door inside his home and entering.

Zack thinks about what he has just done. *I'm sorry, but I must find my parents, and I'm not going to let anyone stop me.*

He enters the house as quietly as possible. There is a short hall-way before him, with three different paths. On the closest path to the left, there is a bathroom, on the farthest path to the left is the laundry room, and the path to the right leads to the kitchen. There is a small wall right next to the door that he hides behind as soon as he closes the door behind him. He peeks around the wall to see the soldier in the kitchen facing the window outside. The dining room table stands between the soldier and the window, and behind the soldier is the living room. To the soldier's right is a longer hallway that leads to two bedrooms; Zack's is on the right while the parents' is on the left. There are many pictures adorning the hallway of the family, from his parents' wedding up to Zack's graduation from high school. Zack quietly moves toward the soldier and hides behind the bar full of drawers and cabinets in front of him. From here, he can just barely see into the living room, but unfortunately, he cannot see the two soldiers inside. However, he can hear them talking to each other. He sneaks forward, making sure not to alert the guard in front of him, and hides behind a small wall that partially separates the living room from the kitchen. He peeks around the wall and sees the two guards with their backs turned to him, looking out the large window in the living room. Quietly, he sneaks past all three guards, taking quick glances at the guards as he does so to make sure that they don't turn around. Thankfully, they don't, and Zack is able to sneak by them without being spotted. He walks through the hallway, hugging the left wall the entire time, until he comes to the doorway leading into his room. He quickly peeks through to see if there are any guards and sees none. Everything looks exactly how it did when he moved out, with his bed up against the middle of the right wall, a shelf to the right of the bed containing dozens of books, a ceiling fan above the bed, and two closets along the left wall, one containing dozens of board games while the other contains the vacuum cleaner. Zack switches to the right side of the hallway, once again hugging the wall, and continues along the hallway until he reaches his parents' bedroom. He peeks inside but sees nobody. This room also looks exactly the same as when he left, with the bed pushed along the center of the right wall, a large cabinet containing six drawers along the back wall, two small end tables on each side of the bed, each containing two drawers and an alarm clock on top, a very wide cabinet along the wall next to the hallway containing a large mirror and about a dozen drawers, a large window looking outside along the back wall, a closet on far side of the left wall, and a bathroom on the near side of the left wall. Zack sneaks in, looking for his parents, so he looks in the bathroom and sees nobody, then looks in the closet and once again sees nobody.

Where are my parents? Zack thinks to himself. *I'll have to ask one of the guards where they are.*

He leaves his parents' bedroom and sneaks back down the hallway to the kitchen. He peeks into the living room and sees that the two guards are still facing away from him, as is the guard in the kitchen. He sneaks up behind the guard in the kitchen and punches him in the back of the head, knocking him to the floor and rendering him unconscious. The two guards in the living room quickly turn around, as does Zack. Leaping toward them, he punches one guard in the cheek, knocking him down to the ground. He then quickly punches the other guard in the stomach, making the guard fall to his knees. The other guard slowly gets back to his feet, and Zack sweeps his legs, knocking him back to the ground. As the other guard is getting back to his feet, Zack runs around him and wraps his arm around the guard's neck, choking him out and rendering him unconscious after a few seconds. Finally, Zack grabs the other guard off the ground and sits him up, wrapping his arm around the soldier's neck in the process.

Suddenly, the guard's radio goes off, and a guard on the other end of the line asks, "Echo 4, this is Echo 7, checking in. Please respond, over."

Zack tells the guard, "Answer the radio now. And don't try to warn him, otherwise I will snap your neck."

The guard picks up the radio and answers, "Echo 7, this is Echo 4, all clear, over."

The guard on the other end responds, "Roger that, Echo 4, over."

Zack tells the guard, "Now put the radio back."

The guard clips the radio back on his pocket.

Zack says, "Good, now, tell me where to find Alex and Sara Branford."

The guard asks, "Why should I tell you?"

"Because if you don't tell me, I'm going to snap your neck and kill you. You wouldn't want that now, would you?"

"Okay, okay! Alex and Sara Branford were moved to a military base about fifty miles north of here."

"You mean to the Alexandria Military Outpost?"

"Yeah, that's the place."

"Thanks for your help," Zack says as he begins to choke out the guard. After about ten seconds, the guard is knocked out. He then walks out of the house and sneaks past all the guards in the backyard. He reaches the car that he stole and drives off.

After driving for about an hour, Zack finally reaches Alexandria Military Outpost. He stops the car about a mile away and walks the rest of the distance until he is just outside the base. After finding a good position, he spies on the guards in the base, watching their patrol patterns and counting how many there are. He tries to find a hole in their patrols that he can use to sneak past them but finds none.

I'm not going to get inside without confrontation, he thinks to himself. *I'm going to have to take out many of the guards in order to get inside.*

He spends several minutes formulating a strategy in order to get inside undetected. He comes up with several ideas, but most of them wouldn't work. Finally, he develops a strategy that he thinks will work.

He runs toward the base until he starts to get close, then he becomes more careful, waiting for opening in the patrols of the guards in the watchtowers on his side of the base. When he sees an opening, he rushes forward and takes cover behind bushes and trees whenever a guard is about to spot him. After several minutes of this, he makes it to the fence surrounding the facility. He grabs the fence with both hands and tears it apart, creating a hole wide enough for him to crawl through.

Now inside the base, he quickly takes cover behind a nearby parked jeep, being as quiet as he can while doing so. He peeks around the jeep and watches the patrols for several minutes, at which point a guard gets close to his position. As soon as the guard turns his back, Zack sneaks up behind him and chokes him unconscious. Zack drags the soldier's unconscious body behind the jeep and puts the soldier's clothing on. He then walks out from behind the jeep and deeper into the base, extremely nervous the entire way.

I really hope this works, Zack thinks. *I can't possibly take on the entire base by myself.*

He wanders through the base, trying to act normal to attract as little attention as possible. He makes his way through the barracks and the mess hall until he finds what he is looking for, the holding cells.

He searches through the holding cells for several minutes until he finds his parents, making sure not to let them see him to make sure they don't say anything and attract suspicion. A tall guard notices him and walks up to him, asking, "Who are you and what are you doing here?"

Zack answers, "I'm…Private John Smith, sir. I was recently assigned to this base, and my commanding officer told me to patrol here."

"I wasn't told of any new recruits being assigned here. Who's your commanding officer?"

"Um…" Zack says before rushing forward and punching the guard in the face, knocking him unconscious immediately. He then searches the guard and finds a keycard before hiding the guard's unconscious body out of sight. He walks back to his parents' cell and swipes the keycard in the reader next to the door. The reader beeps twice, and the door opens.

Alex and Sara are sitting together on a bench, and when Zack opens the door, they both turn their heads to the door and watch Zack walk in.

"Who are you, and what did you do to the guard?" Sara asks as Zack walks in.

Zack answers, "It's me, Mom. It's Zack."

"Zack? Is it really you?"

"Yes, Mom. It's me."

"What are you doing here?"

"I came to see you."

Alex interjects, "Son, it's good to see you, but you shouldn't have come here. What if somebody finds out who you are?"

Zack answers, "Don't worry, Dad, I have everything under control."

"Did you kill that guard?"

"Relax, Dad, I just knocked him out. He'll be fine."

"Oh, that's good to hear."

Sara says, "Oh, son, it's so good to see you."

Zack replies, "It's good to see you too, Mom and Dad. What happened to you? Why are you here? Have they been treating you well?"

"Yes, they have been treating us very well. Don't you worry about that."

"I'm glad to hear that. But what exactly happened? Why are you here?"

"It happened a few days ago. Some soldiers came to our house and told us to come with them. Then they took us here."

"I see. They didn't want you to talk to me."

"But why? What's going on?"

"Mom…Dad…are you my real parents?"

There is a long pause before Alex finally answers, "No, son, we are not your real parents. We found you abandoned in a ditch when you were just a baby. I'm sorry we never told you."

Zack replies, "It's okay. I understand."

Sara cuts in, "Oh, son. I'm so sorry."

Zack responds, "It's okay, really."

Alex interjects again, "Now that that's out of the way, would you mind telling us what's going on?"

Zack answers, "Mom, Dad, do you remember what the seraph are?"

"You mean the alien race that used to live on this planet?"

"Yeah."

"Yeah, I remember learning about them in school. Do you remember, honey?"

Sara answers, "Yeah, I remember learning about them. Why do you ask?"

Zack says, "Because…I am a seraph."

Both Sara and Alex's expressions turn to shock, and at the same time, they both exclaim, "What?"

"It's true," Zack says, "I am a seraph."

Alex replies, "But I thought all of the seraph were captured at the end of the war all those years ago."

"All of them were, except one. My mother. She managed to escape."

"But how do you know this?"

"Another seraph told me."

"Told you? How is that possible? I thought they were all frozen."

"They were, until I let one of them out."

"What? You let one of them out? Why would you do that?"

"I don't know. I really don't. In fact, I don't even remember doing it. It's like I blacked out."

"Zack…are you okay? This sounds really serious. I think you might be delusional."

"I'm not delusional. This is all true."

"I'm sorry, it's just so hard to believe."

"Look, I don't blame you for having a hard time believing. Hell, I wouldn't believe it myself if I weren't there. But it's true. All of it."

"So you're a seraph, huh? What's it like?"

"I don't feel any different than when I thought I was human."

"How long have you known you were a seraph?"

"I actually just found out a few hours ago. I was in the hospital, and one of the seraph attacked and told me."

"You were in the hospital? Are you okay? What happened?"

"Well, it's kind of a long story, but I'm fine, I promise."

"What about this seraph attack? Were you hurt?"

"No, I wasn't hurt in the seraph attack. Believe me, I'm fine."

"Okay. You know I'm just looking out for you, don't you?"

"Yes, I know, and I'm grateful, but you don't need to worry. I can handle myself. I was in the army."

"I know, but you're my son, even if we didn't actually birth you. You know that, right? You will always be our son."

"Yes, I know. Thank you, Mom, Dad."

Sara says, "Come here, son."

Zack walks over to Sara and gives her a hug, then he turns and gives Alex a hug as well.

"I love you both," Zack says.

Sara replies, "And we love you."

Alex adds, "We will always love you, son."

Zack responds, "I have to leave now. I'm sorry I can't take you with me, but there's something important I have to do."

"We understand, son," Sara says.

"I'll miss you guys."

"And we'll miss you too."

Zack leaves the room and closes the door behind him. The lock reactivates as soon as the door shuts all the way, locking Sara and Alex in the room. He then quickly leaves the area with the holding cells and heads back toward the area of the fence that he opened.

However, along the way, the facility's alarm goes off. A voice comes over the loudspeakers that says, "Alert, there is an intruder in the base. All nonessential personnel, to your quarters immediately."

Zack quickens his pace toward the fence; however, along the way, he is stopped by a large soldier, who tells him, "Soldier, return to your quarters, now."

Zack then turns around and heads toward the barracks. He runs straight past the entrance to the barracks and heads to the back. There, he sees two guards patrolling the area. He waits till both guards pass each other and sneaks past them without alerting either of them. Looking for potential exit points along the way, he continues making his way through the base. Finally, he reaches the edge of the base, where there are two more guards on patrol, along with two guards in nearby watchtowers looking out over the outer edge of the base. Zack quickly runs up behind one of the guards and chokes him out quietly, then does the same to the other guard on patrol and hides both of their unconscious bodies. He then sneaks up to the fence and tears a hole in it large enough for him to crawl through as quietly as possible. Looking up at the guards in the watchtowers, he waits until they are both looking away from him before sneaking out of the base, hiding behind trees and shrubbery whenever necessary to avoid being spotted.

He eventually makes it far enough from the base to no longer require hiding and makes the long trek around to reach the vehicle he came in on. *I need to find my mother,* he thinks to himself. *I need to find her and ask her where she's been my whole life and why she abandoned me.* He eventually reaches the vehicle he came in on and drives away from the base.

After about half an hour, he has a vision in his mind of the woman from his dreams. She tells him, *Zack, we need to meet. Meet me at the following coordinates.* She then gives him a set of coordinates to find her at.

CHAPTER 16

ZACK TYPES THE coordinates into the car's GPS and drives to them. They lead to a secluded forest in the middle of nowhere, the perfect place to have a conversation in private. Zack parks the car outside the forest and heads in, not knowing what to expect.

This is the woman from my dreams, Zack thinks. *Could she possibly be my mother?*

He walks deep into the forest, looking everywhere for the woman the entire way. After about fifteen minutes of walking, he finds the woman standing in the middle of a clearing, waiting for him.

"You made it," she begins. "I'm so glad to see you again." Her voice is soft and velvety smooth.

Zack replies, "You can speak to me in my mind, since you're obviously another seraph. Are you my real mother?"

"I am. It is so good to see you again, my son."

"If you're so glad to see me, then why did you abandon me? Why did you leave me all alone?"

"But you weren't alone. Sara and Alex found you and took you in and loved you like you were their own child."

"Yes, but that still doesn't explain why you left."

"Believe me, my son, I didn't want to leave you. You were the most precious thing in the world to me."

"Then why did you leave me?"

"I had no choice. You must believe me."

"But you still haven't told me why."

"Because I was on the run. You see, the government knows that I survived the war and escaped custody, and they've been hunting me ever since. I couldn't risk them finding you, so I left you somewhere they wouldn't find you. I'm so sorry, but believe me, it was incredibly painful leaving you behind."

"But wait, how have you survived this long?"

"We seraph have an extraordinarily long life span. We can live up to five hundred years."

"So how old was I when you abandoned me?"

"You were a little over a year old. We seraph grow at the same rate as normal humans until we reach adulthood, at which point our aging slows drastically. That's how you were able to pass as a human."

"So who was my father?"

"Your father was a great man. He was killed in the war, but he was very brave. He died protecting you and me."

"So have you been contacting me in my dreams all this time? I've been having dreams about you at random points."

"Yes, I have been keeping my eye on you, making sure you were safe."

"What about when I was in the military? You just let me join, knowing how dangerous it was?"

"I knew that you would be safe. You are so much stronger than a normal person. I had faith that you would survive, which is why I did nothing when I saw you join the military."

"All right. But what about the other seraph? He told me that he talked to you."

"You mean Alistair? Yes, he did come to see me. He wanted me to join him in living a life together, but I said no."

"So Alistair is his name, huh? Speaking of names, I'm afraid I still don't know yours."

"My name is Mycenea."

"So why did you say no to Alistair? Why didn't you want to live out the rest of your life with him?"

"The truth is, I've become used to living alone. It's how I've lived most of my life, so I don't really want to live with anyone."

"So why did you call me here?"

"Because you are my son, and I wanted to see you. It has been years, and I wanted to see how you've grown with my own eyes."

"Well, here I am. Now what?"

"Now you have a choice to make. I'm sure Alistair gave you the same offer he gave me, to live with him."

"What, you didn't see that? Can't you detect my thoughts or something?"

"Usually I can, but I couldn't then. Whenever you would get those headaches, it was me trying to protect you from coming under Alistair's influence. At the hospital, he was finally able to break through my defense and talk to you in your mind. At that point, I was no longer able to sense your thoughts."

"Do you know that I was the one who freed Alistair in the first place?"

"Yes. I was trying to protect you then, but I was unable to. He was able to take control of your body through sheer force of will and forced you to free him. I was, however, able to mask your brainwaves from him just enough that he didn't know who it was that he was controlling."

"So that's how it happened. But then, how did he find out that I am a seraph?"

"I don't know. You'll have to ask him yourself."

There is a long pause before Mycenea continues, "So have you decided what you are going to do now?"

Zack answers, "No, not yet. What do you think I should do?"

"I think you should do what your heart tells you."

"Gee, thanks. That's real helpful."

"I'm serious. You need to listen to your heart and follow it. This isn't a choice that I can make for you. You have to decide what to do for yourself."

"All right, thanks."

"Zack?"

"Yeah?"

"Can you come here and give me a hug?"

"Okay."

Zack walks over to Mycenea and hugs her. While they're hugging, she says, "It's so good to see you again, my son."

Zack replies, "And it's good to see you, Mother."

"I'm so sorry that I abandoned you. I just wanted you to be able to live a normal life."

"It's okay. I understand."

"Thank you, my son."

The two then stop hugging, and Zack takes a few seconds to collect his thoughts. He then asks, "So what happens between us now?"

Mycenea answers, "Whatever you want, my son. If you want to continue to see me, then we can meet again. If not, I would completely understand."

Zack takes a few seconds before answering, "I would like to see you again. You are my mother, after all."

"That makes me so happy to hear you say that. In that case, I will call you again when I'm available."

"I would like that."

"But for now, we must depart. You have an important decision to make, and I want you to have as much time as you need to think it over."

"All right. I'll see you again mother."

Zack and Mycenea part ways, and Zack returns to his vehicle. He drives away from the woods and takes time to think over what he wants to do. After a while, Zack gets a vision in his head of Alistair, who says to Zack, *Come and meet me at the following coordinates.* Alistair then gives Zack a set of coordinates to find him at.

CHAPTER 17

ZACK INPUTS THE coordinates in the car's GPS and drives to them as quickly as he can. They lead to a cave about fifty miles away from his home. He parks the car just outside the cave and slowly walks inside, watching his back at every opportunity, just in case Alistair tries to attack him again. After several minutes of walking, Zack stumbles upon a large opening, with a hole in the ceiling, allowing for light to shine through and lighting up the whole area. Standing in the middle of this opening is Alistair, still wearing the same clothing as before, staring at Zack as he enters.

"Welcome, Zack. I've been expecting you," Alistair greets Zack.

"I know, you called me here," Zack responds.

"So have you changed your mind about my proposal?"

"I have not. How did you know I was a seraph? I spoke with Mycenea, and she told me that she shielded my brainwaves from you, so you shouldn't have been able to tell it was me."

"I didn't know it was you that I took control of. I actually went to that hospital with the intention of killing you. I didn't find out that you were a seraph until after I walked into your room and saw the x-ray photos of you. One of them showed your brain, and I saw that you had the brain of a seraph. Then I put two and two together and found out that you were the one who freed me. I thank you for that, by the way."

"Well, you know that I didn't do it intentionally, right?"

"I do. But still, I must express my gratitude that you did."

"Well, you're welcome, I guess."

"So you haven't reconsidered my offer. That's a shame."

"I'm sorry, but I can't just abandon the life I've built for myself. Not after I worked so hard for everything I have."

"So what do you want to do now?"

"I've come to fulfill my mission."

"Your mission?"

"Yes. The mission I was given by a good friend of mine. I was to find all of the captive seraph and recapture them. And that's what I've come to do."

"Yet you came unarmed. Bold choice."

"I didn't have time to find a weapon. But that's okay. I can take you even without any weapons."

"I'd like to see you try."

"Oh, believe me, I've picked up a number of tricks during my time in the military. I won't lose to you."

"We shall see about that."

"Then let's end this."

"Yes, let's."

Alistair unsheathes his sword and rushes toward Zack. He quickly swipes at Zack with his sword, but Zack is able to deftly dodge the attack. Alistair then thrusts his sword toward Zack, but he sidesteps the strike. Zack then tries to counter with a punch to Alistair's gut, but Alistair blocks the blow and kicks Zack straight in the groin. Zack recoils from the blow, and Alistair takes the opportunity to swipe at him with his sword, but Zack ducks underneath the strike and counters by grabbing Alistair's right arm, twisting it, and punching down the back of his elbow, breaking Alistair's arm and causing him to howl in pain. Seizing the opportunity, Zack then grabs the sword as Alistair drops it. Now wielding the sword, Zack immediately swipes several times at Alistair, who dodges most of the attacks but gets slashed across the chest with the final strike, causing blood to shoot out of the wound. Zack then takes the opportunity to go for the finishing blow, but Alistair manages to avoid his thrust. Alistair then quickly snaps his arm back into place, letting out a sharp cry of pain as he does. Zack tries once again to finish Alistair off, but Alistair grabs Zack's wrist as Zack attempts to swipe at him.

"Your skills are quite impressive," Alistair begins. "I see now how you were able to kill my other two brethren. But don't think that you can stand a chance against me, boy. I was fighting before you were born."

Zack retorts, "I won't let you get away with what you've done. You almost killed a good friend of mine."

"You mean the woman?"

"Yes."

"I see, then after I kill you, I'll just have to pay her a visit next."

"No! I won't let you hurt her!"

"You won't be able to stop me once you're dead!"

"I'll stop you right now!"

Zack quickly jerks his hand free of Alistair's grasp then swipes furiously at Alistair, who dodges all the attacks.

Alistair begins taunting Zack, "Yes, strike at me with all your hatred!"

Zack yells, "I'll kill you!"

Alistair punches Zack straight in the gut, then with no wasted motion, quickly grabs Zack's arm and pulls the sword out of his hand. He then shoves Zack to the ground and, standing over him, raises the sword to deliver the final, killing blow. However, Zack quickly recovers and sweeps Alistair's legs, knocking him to the ground. Zack then grabs Alistair's arm and slams it against the ground several times until Alistair lets go of the sword. As Alistair is laying on the ground, Zack grabs the sword and plunges it straight into Alistair's chest, causing blood to seep out of Alistair's mouth.

As he lies dying, Alistair says, "Congratulations on defeating me and ensuring the end of our species. I hope you're proud of yourself."

Zack responds, "No, I'm not proud at all of what happened here."

"Goodbye, cruel world," Alistair says as he breathes his last and his body goes limp.

CHAPTER 18

ZACK LOOKS OVER the corpse of his fallen adversary for several seconds before saying, "I'm sorry, but you left me no choice." He then pulls the sword out of Alistair's body and leaves the cave the same way he came.

Outside of the cave, he sees about a dozen soldiers, all pointing assault rifles at him, with Miller in the back.

"Whoa, hold up," Zack begins. "The seraph is dead. You can put your weapons down."

Miller replies, "Really? Did you kill him?"

"Yes, I did."

"Why?"

"To finish what I started. Plus, he tried to kill me at the hospital."

"Men, go into the cave to confirm that what Zack says is true. But be careful, it could be a trap."

"I assure you, it's no trap. The seraph is dead."

"We shall see."

The soldiers all run around Zack and enter the cave. Zack notices that Amanda is among them. After several minutes, the soldiers return from the cave with the corpse of Alistair in tow.

"We found it, sir," one of the soldiers says as they lay the body down at Miller's feet. He then turns to Zack and says, "What should we do about him?"

Miller takes out his radio and calls in, saying, "This is Miller, the escaped seraph is dead. However, Zack is here as well. What do you want us to do with him?"

The voice on the other end of the line, a female voice, says, "He is a criminal and a threat. Bring him in."

Miller puts the radio away and tells Zack, "Well, you heard her. I need to take you in, Zack."

Zack replies, "Miller, we're friends. Can't you just let me go?"

"I'm afraid not. I need to bring you in."

Zack thinks, *Wait a minute…I'm a seraph, and what they did to the other seraph…*

Miller says, "Don't do anything stupid, Zack."

Zack asks, "What are you going to do with me once you bring me in?"

"I don't know. That's up to the council to decide."

"What do you think they'll do?"

"I don't know, probably throw you in prison."

"I don't think so."

"What do you mean?"

"Think about it. I'm a seraph. And what did they do to the other seraph?"

"They experimented on them."

"Right. Which is exactly what they are going to do with me."

"You don't know that."

"Oh, but I do. They're going to perform cruel experiments on me, and I refuse to be anyone's lab rat."

"What are you doing, Zack?"

"I'm doing what I must." Zack rushes forward with his sword raised, intending to kill his friend.

"Fire!" Miller shouts at the soldiers.

The soldiers open fire on Zack, all except Amanda, who refuses to shoot him. The bullets riddle Zack's body until he is knocked to the ground, lying in a pool of blood.

Miller walks over to Zack and says, "It didn't have to be this way."

Zack coughs up blood and replies, "I had…no choice. I wasn't going to let you experiment on me."

"You don't know that that's what they were going to do."

"But I do. It's what they did to the other seraph."

"Zack, I'm so sorry about this."

"So am I, old friend, so am I…" Zack says as he lets out his final breath.

CHAPTER 19

MYCENEA SNAPS BACK to herself after having watched Zack get gunned down. She begins sobbing profusely and lets out a sharp cry of pain. After regaining her composure, her sadness turns to anger and hatred, and she thinks to herself, *I will make them pay for what they have done. I will kill them all!*

ABOUT THE AUTHOR

CRAIG UNGRUHN IS from a small town in Ohio, where he currently lives with his family. He is a graduate of Wright State University, where he got a bachelor's degree in business management. He loves fantasy and science fiction, and enjoys playing video games, watching television, watching YouTube videos, and reading comic books.

CPSIA information can be obtained
at www.ICGtesting.com
Printed in the USA
LVHW020921030721
691627LV00001B/29